He looked dow

'Betsy must be here
stiffly.

'That is so ridiculous,' Meg said. 'We're not alone—Jeannie is here with us.'

'Jeannie is only a child,' Adam returned curtly.

'And you are a man and I am a woman,' Meg flung back at him. 'Does that mean we are not to be trusted to be alone together?'

His eyes were very dark. 'You are right in that, Meg,' he said quietly. 'You are a young woman, and a bonny one. And people would talk.'

Elisabeth Scott was born in Scotland, but has lived in South Africa for many years. Happily married, with four children and grandchildren, she has always been interested in reading and writing about medical instances. Her middle daughter is a midwifery sister, and is Elisabeth's consultant on both medical authenticity and on how nurses feel and react. Her daughter wishes she met more doctors like the ones her mother writes about!

Recent titles by the same author:

HAPPY CHRISTMAS, DOCTOR DEAR

WANTED: A MOTHER

BY
ELISABETH SCOTT

MILLS & BOON®

All the characters in this book have no existence outside the imagination of the author, and have no relation whatsoever to anyone bearing the same name or names. They are not even distantly inspired by any individual known or unknown to the author, and all the incidents are pure invention.

*First published in Great Britain 1999
Harlequin Mills & Boon Limited,
Eton House, 18-24 Paradise Road, Richmond, Surrey TW9 1SR*

© Elisabeth Scott 1999

ISBN 0 263 81517 X

*Set in Times Roman 10 on 11½ pt.
03-9903-53586-D*

*Printed and bound in Norway
by AIT Trondheim AS, Trondheim*

CHAPTER ONE

'COME on, Meg, you're a nurse, not a nursemaid. And in the depths of some Scottish glen? Who on earth could you meet there? Meaning men. Salt, please.'

Meg passed the salt across the table of the hospital cafeteria.

'Right now I don't want to meet anyone, particularly men, Lindy,' she said with perfect truth.

Her friend's dark eyes filled with sympathetic tears.

'Oh, Meg, love, I'm so sorry, but you really do need to get out there and see that it isn't every man who's an absolute— I was working with him in Theatre the other day and, I tell you, when he said, "Scalpel, Nurse," he just about got it where he'd really feel it. Rat!'

Meg shrugged. Convincingly, she hoped.

'He met someone else, Lindy, that's all.'

Lindy sniffed. 'Someone whose father just happens to be on the hospital board.'

Meg looked down at the white band on her left hand, where Dr Simon Teale's diamond ring had been until two months ago. 'I'm just glad it happened before we were any further into wedding plans,' she said quietly.

Lindy finished her salad, and put down her knife and fork.

'I still say he's a rat,' she said firmly. 'OK, tell me more about this job.'

'I don't know much more,' Meg replied. 'I'm seeing this Scottish farmer tomorrow. He has a small daughter who's been ill, and he needs someone to look after her. Jane Peyton on Men's Surgical told me about the job—he's some sort of second cousin or something, and he asked her if she knew anyone who might be interested.'

She looked at her watch.

'Time I was back on duty,' she said, and stood up.

It was a busy afternoon on Women's Surgical, and she was glad of that—first because being busy meant having no time to think, and second because she really enjoyed the busyness and the bustle of the surgical ward. There were two new hysterectomy patients from the morning's theatre list, a Mrs Brown and a Miss Hilton, as well as Barbara Jennings, a gastric-resection with respiratory problems and young Ashley Cooper, who had just had an emergency appendicectomy. Half a dozen patients were recovering from more routine surgery. And old Mrs Smith had an unexpected haemorrhage just as Meg was going off duty.

Lindy's right, she thought. I'm a nurse, not a nursemaid. Maybe I'm making a mistake, even thinking about this job. I suppose I'd better go through with the interview, though.

Within five minutes of meeting Adam Kerr in the lounge of the nurses' home it was all too obvious that she wasn't the only one who thought this was a mistake.

He was standing at the window when she went in.

'Mr Kerr? Sister Home said you were here. I'm Meg Bennett.'

The man at the window turned. He was tall and dark, and his polite smile sort of froze, Meg thought. As did his outstretched hand. In a moment he recovered, but his dark brows drew together.

'I didn't realise you were so young,' he said, without preamble.

Meg felt warm colour flood her cheeks. 'I'm twenty-four,' she said, and she lifted her chin. 'I'm a fully qualified nurse, Mr Kerr. I thought Jane Peyton would have told you that.'

'She did,' Adam Kerr returned, 'but I expected someone older.'

I will not, Meg told herself, lose my cool.

'Does that make a difference, Mr Kerr?' she asked, as pleasantly as she could.

He shrugged. 'I can't see a girl like you fitting in well in a lonely farmhouse in a quiet glen miles from what you would call civilisation,' he said.

'I don't see how you can know anything of what sort of person I am,' Meg said, and she knew there were bright flags of anger in her cheeks. 'As it happens, Mr Kerr, I grew up on a farm in Devon. But I'm sure you're right— you would be better off looking for someone older. I'm sorry I've— I'm sorry we've wasted each other's time.'

She had the satisfaction of seeing the disapproval on his lean brown face give way to surprise before she turned and left the room.

Well, she thought, I certainly couldn't see myself working for him!

It still seemed a good idea—leaving the hospital, getting right away—and she would have to do some serious thinking about that, she knew. Maybe she would write to Amy Carter who'd taken a job in Dubai.

However, a few days later, before she could do that, she had just come off duty, hurried back to her room and washed her hair when one of the first-year nurses knocked on her door.

'Sister Home asked me to tell you there's someone to see you,' she said. 'Could you come down?'

Meg wound the towel round her head and cast a swift glance at herself in the mirror. Tracksuit, bare feet, newly washed hair. Probably Mum taking the chance of someone coming up to London to send me some cake and biscuits, she thought, and she thrust her feet into sandals so that whoever it was wouldn't go back and tell her mother about the bare feet on the cold floor.

'Hi,' she said brightly, as she went in to the big sunny room. 'Did my mum—?' She stopped.

'Good afternoon, Nurse Bennett,' Adam Kerr said, his eyes taking in the tracksuit and the towel.

There was some small satisfaction in realising that he seemed to feel as awkward as she did.

'Can we sit down?' he asked, and Meg managed to nod.

'I'll come straight to the point,' he said brusquely, and she wondered if he ever did anything else. 'Nurse Bennett, would you reconsider taking the job as Jeannie's nurse? I…haven't been able to find anyone else willing to come. I spoke to Jane Peyton again and she said perhaps I should come back to you.'

There was no anger or disapproval now in the big man's dark eyes—only, Meg realised with wonder, something close to a plea for help. A plea she couldn't ignore.

'Tell me about your daughter, Mr Kerr,' she said quietly.

'Jeannie is ten,' Adam Kerr said, then added baldly, 'She has leukaemia. I've had her at a clinic in Switzerland, and then we went to America. She's had chemotherapy and she's in remission at the moment, but Dr Roland in Boston says there is nothing more that can be done. Jeannie wants…' He stopped. Then, with careful control, he went on.

'Jeannie wants to go home to the glen,' he said. 'She doesn't know how serious her illness is, and I don't want her to know. She's talking about going back to the glen school, and she will be able to do that for the moment. But there will be times, and I can't say how soon that will be, when she will need nursing. I have a housekeeper at the farm, but she's not young and she isn't a nurse. That's why I need you.'

'Jeannie's mother?' Meg asked.

'She died when Jeannie was three. A car accident,' Adam Kerr said briefly. He leaned forward. 'I'm sorry about what I said the other day, Nurse Bennett. When I thought about it afterwards I realised I was very rude. And perhaps it would be better for Jeannie to have someone young and bright around. What do you think? Could you take the job?'

It wasn't easy to reply.

'I don't know,' Meg said at last, honestly. 'I do want to get away from the hospital, make a change, but I'm not sure this is the sort of change I should be thinking about.'

'Why do you want to get away?' Adam Kerr asked unexpectedly.

Meg didn't give herself time to think about her reply.

'Because I've just been jilted,' she said as lightly as she could, 'and I'm getting very tired of people either being sympathetic or downright nosy! That's how hospitals are.'

'I'm sorry,' Adam Kerr said. Then, to her relief, he left the subject. 'Won't you at least give it a try, Nurse Bennett? Come with Jeannie and me to Glen Mor.'

Afterwards, Meg couldn't believe she had made the decision just like that.

'All right, I'll come,' she said. 'But, Mr Kerr, you'd better not call me Nurse or Jeannie will wonder about that. Make it Meg.'

He looked quite different when he smiled, she realised as Adam Kerr's face lit up. He agreed, and said he had already talked to Jeannie about having someone to come and live with them to keep her company. Would she call him Adam? he said. Within ten minutes, Meg realised later, a little dazed, they had discussed the practicalities. As it happened, she was due three weeks' holiday, and if Matron was sympathetic and counted that as part of her notice she could be ready to leave with Adam Kerr and his daughter at the end of the week.

*   *   *

Very early on Saturday morning Meg and two large suitcases were ready outside the nurses' home when a fairly old Land Rover drew up.

'Hello, Meg,' Adam Kerr said, climbing out. Then, not hiding his surprise, he added, 'You look different.'

Well, Meg thought, considering I was in uniform the first time you saw me and in a tracksuit with a towel round my hair the next time, that figures. She caught sight of her reflection in the window. She was wearing jeans and a thick jersey because this early on a morning in February it was pretty cold. Her short brown curls had been brushed a little too hastily, she saw.

'I thought we'd said I wouldn't be wearing uniform,' she said defensively.

'Of course,' he replied. 'But you look even younger.'

Meg took a deep breath. 'If you want to change your mind, Mr Kerr—Adam—this is the time to do it,' she said.

'I'm sorry,' Adam Kerr said. 'I'll put your cases in. I'm afraid my Land Rover is pretty old and her springs aren't too good, specially after sitting around my cousin's place for six months. Do you mind sitting in the back?'

'Not at all,' Meg replied as she climbed up. 'And this is Jeannie. Hello.'

The little girl in the front seat had fair hair, held back in an Alice band, and grey eyes. She must be like her mother, Meg thought, and then Jeannie smiled. Her smile was Adam Kerr's smile, lighting up her small face just as his had done. She returned Meg's greeting softly and Meg couldn't help a swift and professional assessment, relieved to find that, apart from being pale, she didn't look ill.

Jeannie wasn't a chatterbox, Meg found during the long journey, but when her father mentioned that they'd gone to Disneyworld, and Meg said that she had been there too, there was plenty to talk about.

'I liked the World of Dolls best, I think,' Jeannie said

seriously. 'Wasn't it lovely, in the little boat, seeing all the dolls and hearing them sing? Daddy liked the Swiss Family Robinson bit best, didn't you, Daddy?'

Adam agreed with that, and Meg said she wasn't sure whether for her it had been the World of Dolls or the journey to the Never-Never Land.

Later they stopped for something to eat and then, when Jeannie was sleepy, she and Meg changed places, and Meg tucked the travelling rug around her. Adam didn't seem to feel the need to make conversation, and she was glad of that. After a while, when they had almost reached Perth, she asked him when they would reach the glen.

'We should be there before nine,' he told her. 'I'm sorry we're just pushing on, but I said we'd arrive today. Betsy will have something ready for us, I know.'

He told her, his voice level and matter-of-fact, that when he'd decided to look for further help for Jeannie he'd let his farm, but he had written from America to say he was coming back.

'Betsy—Betsy Cameron, my housekeeper—was staying on, and although William Craig will have left last week Betsy will have everything ready for us.'

He glanced at her.

'You're tired, Meg,' he said. 'Have a sleep. It will help to pass the time.'

Meg assured him that she wasn't sleepy, but it was quite pleasant to sit with her eyes closed. Although left to her thoughts, she couldn't hold back some of the more disturbing ones. What, in fact, had she let herself in for, coming to a lonely glen to look after a little girl who might at any time be very ill indeed? And that little girl's father was a man who wasn't too good at hiding his misgivings about her suitability for the job. I've said I'll give it a try, and I'm not going back on that, Meg told herself firmly. And that's that.

She looked out of the window, but it was dark and the lights of the few oncoming cars had a hypnotic effect. She closed her eyes. Some time later she woke to hear Jeannie saying excitedly, 'If it was light we'd see the sea, wouldn't we, Daddy?'

'Yes, we would,' her father replied. 'And now we go over the old bridge into the glen.'

'Can I tell Meg about the bridge, Daddy?' Jeannie said. Without waiting for a reply, she said, 'It was built by General Wade, Meg, after the '45. There weren't any good roads or bridges before that, and people said if you'd seen this road before it was made you'd lift up your hands and bless General Wade.'

'More Irish than Scottish, but you get the meaning,' Adam said. 'We're in Glen Mor now, Meg—this is the village.'

'There's my school, Meg,' Jeannie said, pointing to a stone building, 'and the church and the doctor's house. And Colin lives over there—Colin Cameron's my friend. Hurry, Daddy, we're almost home, and I can't wait to see Glen.' She turned to Meg, her small face bright. 'Glen's my dog, Meg. He's a collie, and he's the best sheepdog in all the glen—he's called Glen because he was born in the glen, you see.'

Adam swung the Land Rover into a farm road, and Meg saw a sign that said CRAIGRANNOCH.

'Funny,' he said, frowning. 'No lights.'

'Maybe the electricity has broken down,' Jeannie suggested. 'It sometimes does, Meg, but we always have candles ready.'

Adam drew up and switched off the engine. For a moment the scudding clouds parted, and there was enough moonlight to reveal the farmhouse, large and square and solid.

'Stay there,' Adam said brusquely, and he took a torch

from the cubby hole. He climbed out, and the beam of the torch shone towards the house. For a moment the light shone downwards, then up again.

'Daddy's getting the key we hide at the side of the porch,' Jeannie said. 'He'll switch on the lights when he opens the door.'

A moment later the lights went on, and Adam strode out.

'Let's get into the house,' he said, and he lifted Jeannie out. Meg scrambled down and followed them into the house along a long passage and into the kitchen. But a cold and cheerless kitchen. There was a large Aga at the far side, but no comforting and welcoming heat came from it.

'I don't know what the heck is wrong,' Adam said tightly, and his dark brows were drawn together. 'Betsy should be here—and the dog.'

'Daddy,' Jeannie said shakily.

Her grey eyes were wide, and all the colour had left her small face.

'Glen's basket is gone,' she said. 'It always stays here beside the stove. Where can he be, Daddy?'

The big man knelt down and put his arms around his small daughter.

'I don't know, lass,' he said, and now there was nothing but gentleness in his voice. 'I don't know where Betsy is, and I don't know where Glen is. But I'll find out.'

Meg's throat was tight. The love and the tenderness in Adam's face, the gentleness of his arms around his small daughter, dispersed her dismay at the strangeness of their arrival at the farm.

There were things to be done, and she could deal with that.

'Adam,' she said quietly, 'Jeannie must be tired and hungry—I know I am. Can I find us something to eat, do you think?'

Adam stood.

'There should be something in the pantry,' he said. 'I can't understand why Betsy—'

He stopped, and Meg saw that he, too, had seen the stricken look return to Jeannie's face. 'Let's look in the pantry,' he said. He took Jeannie's hand and led the way to a door at the far end of the kitchen. Meg followed him into the pantry and looked around. There was very little on the wide shelves, which were obviously designed to hold generous supplies.

'Well,' she said brightly, 'now we know how old Mother Hubbard felt, don't we, Jeannie?' She stood on tiptoe and reached up. 'Although we're not so bad. Two tins of tomato soup—that should do us.'

'And this,' Adam said, reaching beyond her to the back of the shelf. 'Oatcakes.'

Meg looked at the packet in his hand.

'Oatcakes?' she asked.

'Oatcakes are posh bannocks,' Jeannie said. Surprised, she went on, 'Don't you know what bannocks are, Meg?'

Meg shook her head.

'Bannocks are coarse oatcakes, Meg,' Adam said seriously, but for the first time since she'd met him there was an unexpected hint of humour in his voice and in his dark eyes. 'Let's get the soup heated up, and we'll see what you think of oatcakes. Oh.'

He looked at the cold and silent Aga. However, Meg had already checked out the rest of the kitchen.

'I may not know your oatcakes,' she said briskly, 'but I do know how to use a microwave.'

Jeannie had found a tin opener and a large glass bowl.

'I know how to use the microwave too,' she said. 'Betsy won't touch it, but I heat up milk for cocoa in it.'

Adam left the kitchen, and Jeannie watched as Meg put the soup in the microwave to heat.

'Can you find plates for us, Jeannie?' Meg asked, worried now about the dark shadows under Jeannie's grey eyes.

Jeannie opened the big oak dresser and took out three soup plates and three side plates.

'I think we're ready,' Meg said, when she'd found spoons. Adam came back into the room at that moment, carrying a small heater.

'I've switched the heating on,' he said. 'This will help until it gets going.'

Tomato soup had never tasted better, Meg thought, and she was pleased to see some colour return to Jeannie's cheeks.

'I do like your oatcakes,' she said. 'I've never tasted anything quite like them. What are they made of?'

'Just oatmeal, I think, and something to hold it together,' Adam said vaguely. 'But wait till you taste Betsy's home-made bannocks.'

Meg had found a packet of long-life milk, and she poured some for Jeannie.

'It tastes funny,' Jeannie said, and her small nose wrinkled. 'Not like real milk.'

'I don't like it much either,' Meg agreed, 'but it's all we have so just drink it up, please.'

For a moment Jeannie's grey eyes held hers, and then she sighed—a big, melodramatic sigh—and drank her milk. When she had finished she looked at Meg.

'You're not very big, Meg,' she said thoughtfully, 'but you're quite bossy.'

Taken aback, Meg could do nothing but laugh.

'Now I'm going to be even more bossy,' she said. 'I'm taking you to your room. I know you're big enough to get yourself ready for bed, but tonight I'm going to help you because it's cold and you're tired. All right?'

'All right,' Jeannie agreed. She slid off her chair and put her hand in Meg's. There was something very trusting in the feel of the small hand in hers, something that made Meg feel very glad that she was here with Jeannie and her father—here to do something to help the little girl over the shock of this longed-for homecoming.

She had just got Jeannie into warm pyjamas when Adam appeared at the door, carrying a hot-water bottle. He put it into Jeannie's bed, and she got in right away.

'Goodnight, Meg,' she said sedately and politely. She looked at her father. 'Daddy, we'll look for Glen tomorrow, won't we?'

Meg wondered if Jeannie, too, was aware of her father's momentary hesitation.

'We'll do that, lass,' he agreed.

When they were back down in the kitchen, and Meg had found tea and made some, he said worriedly that he was very much afraid that something had happened to Jeannie's dog.

'The basket gone—as if there wasn't a dog here at all. And how could William Craig be looking after my sheep and my cattle, and him with no working dog? I don't like it, I don't like it at all. And Betsy Cameron would never be leaving this house, and her knowing we were coming home.'

He sounded more Scottish—more Highland, she supposed—here in the glen, on his farm.

She hesitated. He was her employer, after all, and he must be a good ten years older than she was, but he did need to be shaken out of this doom and gloom.

'Adam,' she said clearly, and she could see that the authoritative note in her voice had taken him by surprise. 'Adam, Jeannie said I was bossy, and I'm going to be even more bossy now. You can't do anything tonight—about Betsy or about the dog. You must be exhausted after the long drive today. Go to bed and leave all this until morning. Do you want any more tea?'

With some difficulty, the big man smiled.

'Thank you, Meg, I don't want any more tea. And you are right. I can't do anything tonight. I'll show you your room, but first I'll boil more water in the microwave and fill a hot-water bottle for you. No, don't argue, you'll be needing it.'

'I wasn't going to argue. I was going to thank you,' Meg said.

The room he took her to was next to Jeannie's, and she peeped in on the little girl before she got into bed. Jeannie was sleeping soundly, her cheek pillowed on one small hand. Meg went back to her own room. A bit bleak, she couldn't help thinking, but the bed was comfortable, and with the help of the hot-water bottle and the comfort of the duvet she was soon asleep.

When she woke it took her a moment or two to realise where she was—and to remember their arrival the night before. Her heart sank at the memory of the big chilly kitchen, but she forced herself to go and wash quickly and dress. Jeannie was still asleep, and that was good.

The kitchen door was closed, and when she pushed it open the first thing she saw was that the Aga was burning. Adam was standing beside it. Like her, he was wearing the clothes he had travelled in yesterday, a thick jersey of a dark grey and corduroy trousers. He heard her, and turned.

'Two good things,' he said. 'I've got the stove going, and I remembered that Betsy used to keep bread in the deep-freeze in case we were cut off by the snow. So we can have toast for breakfast. No butter, but I found a jar of Betsy's raspberry jam at the back of the cupboard.'

He looked at her.

'I'm sorry about all this,' he said awkwardly. 'You must be wondering what you've let yourself in for here at Craigrannoch.'

Meg coloured for that was all too true.

'I'll defrost the bread, and make some toast,' she said. 'Jeannie was still asleep.'

Jeannie appeared when Meg had just poured tea for Adam and herself. The dark shadows under Jeannie's eyes had gone, Meg saw with relief. For a moment her eyes met Adam's, and she knew that he'd had the same thought.

'Milk or tea, Jeannie?' Meg asked, and Jeannie said she would have tea.

'Because the milk won't taste so bad when it's in tea,' she said. When she'd had a mug of milky tea and a slice of toast with jam she looked across the big wooden table at her father. 'Actually, Daddy, I don't mind one bit not having porridge. Betsy likes me to have porridge,' she explained to Meg. 'She says it will build me up. Daddy, can we go and look for Glen now?'

Adam rose. 'I'm going to the village right away, Jeannie,' he told her. 'I must find out about Betsy.'

'Meg and me can look for Glen,' Jeannie said eagerly. 'We'll go all round the farm. Maybe he's in the barn if— if Mr Craig wouldn't let him sleep in the house.'

For a moment Adam's dark eyes met Meg's, and she knew that he, too, was thinking that if the dog had been anywhere near he would surely have come when he'd heard the car last night.

'All right, you do that,' he said carefully. To Meg he added, 'I'll be back as quickly as I can.'

Five minutes later he drove off, the old Land Rover taking the farm road with no trouble.

'Right, I'll wash up, and we'll go and look for Glen,' Meg said. 'My goodness, that water your Daddy put on the stove is hot enough already. No, we won't bother drying up—we'll leave the dishes at the side. Jeannie, it looks pretty cold outside. I think you need an extra jersey under your jacket.'

As soon as they were outside Jeannie called for the dog.

'Glen, Glen, come, boy.' She turned to Meg. 'I can't whistle like Daddy does,' she said, 'so I call him with the same sound—like this. Glen, whoo whoo. When I'm older I'll be able to whistle, but he does know the sound.'

Meg hadn't really expected the dog to appear, but in spite of that she was disappointed when they'd made a round of the barn and the outhouses and there was no sign of him. But there were about a dozen hens, scratching around the ground.

'Someone's been here yesterday to feed the hens,' Jeannie said, and she pushed open the door of a huge shed. It was filled, Meg saw, with very large animals.

'Cows?' she asked Jeannie nervously.

'Aye, and that's Fergus the bull at the far end on his own,' Jeannie said. She went close to one of the pens and stroked the inhabitant's nose. 'Hello, Daisy, it's me. I'm back, and I won't ever go away again.' She climbed up on the gate to the stall and peered down. 'And they've got their feed too,' she said.

'They're awfully hairy cows,' Meg said, still nervous in spite of the little girl's ease with the big animals.

'They're Highland cattle,' Jeannie told her. 'They're more shaggy than other cows. Betsy doesn't like them either—she calls them thon big hairy beasts.'

She sighed. 'Glen isn't anywhere, Meg. He would have heard me, and he would have come. Don't you think so?'

'Yes, I do,' Meg agreed. She took Jeannie's small mittened hand in hers. 'Let's go back into the house, Jeannie. We could unpack our suitcases.'

Jeannie's small feet dragged as they went back across the farmyard, but when Meg began to unpack the child sat on the bed, cross-legged, and brightened up.

'That's a pretty dress, Meg,' she said, and she touched the silky folds of the turquoise dress Meg had worn for her engagement party. 'Is that a dress for going to dances?'

'Yes, it is,' Meg replied. And what possessed me to bring it here, I don't know, she thought. For I'm not in the least likely to have any occasion to wear it.

'Oh, you've brought your nurse's uniforms with you, I see,' Jeannie commented.

She had already seen the uniforms so it was too late to do anything but hang them up, Meg realised.

'Oh—you knew I was a nurse?' she asked.

'Well, we came to the hospital to pick you up, didn't we?' Jeannie said reasonably. 'Anyway, Daddy said you were a nurse, and you were wanting to have a change, and that's why you said you would come to the farm with us. To keep me company, Daddy said.' She frowned. 'I'm very fond of Betsy, but she's quite old and she isn't much company for me. I'm glad you came, Meg.'

'I'm glad I came too, Jeannie,' Meg said, more than a little surprised to find that she really meant it.

When her clothes were unpacked and put away they did Jeannie's clothes. Remembering her cousin's little girls, who were much the same age as Jeannie, Meg found it oddly touching to see how careful and tidy Jeannie was with her clothes, folding everything and putting all her underwear and jerseys in neat rows.

'I think maybe all my clothes will fit me again,' Jeannie murmured, holding up a tartan pinafore dress. 'You know, Meg, when I was taking such a lot of pills I got quite fat. Even my face was fat.'

Meg's heart turned over. 'Yes, that does sometimes happen with some kinds of pills, Jeannie,' she said carefully, 'but you had to take them to make you better.'

Jeannie folded a bright blue cardigan and put it in her cupboard.

'Well,' she said, thinking about this, 'actually, I didn't feel very well when I was taking the pills. Sometimes I was really sick. Even after I stopped them I was sometimes

sick.' Her small face brightened. 'But I'm all right now. I
don't get sick. And I'm not fat any more.'

'No, you're certainly not,' Meg agreed. She was in remission, Adam had said. But there was no knowing how
long that would last—there never was. To her professional
eye, Jeannie's skin had a translucent look. And she had
already seen how the dark shadows came under Jeannie's
grey eyes.

But for now she wasn't ill. And they would just have to
take each day as it came.

'There's the Land Rover—Daddy's back,' Jeannie said,
and she hurried out of the room and downstairs. Meg followed her, reaching the kitchen in time to see Adam bending to kiss his daughter.

'We're all unpacked, Daddy, and Meg has a beautiful
dance dress with her,' Jeannie told him.

The big man straightened.

'I don't think you'll be finding much use for a dance
dress here in the glen, Meg,' he said, more than a little
curtly. 'I did tell you how isolated we are here.'

Meg felt her cheeks grow warm.

'I know that,' she replied, probably, she thought, equally
curtly, 'but I had to bring everything with me. My room in
the nurses' home was needed.'

For a moment longer Adam's dark eyes held hers, then
he nodded.

'Of course,' he said politely, but Meg was sure there was
still disapproval on his face. He lifted up a shopping bag.
'Betsy was at her sister's house. I thought I would at least
get news of her there. She came to the shop with me and
we got some food. She'll get whatever else we need, and
I'll pick her up later.'

'But why wasn't she here, waiting for us?' Jeannie asked.
'And—and did you ask her about Glen?'

Adam's face was very still, very bleak.

'She wasn't here, 'he said, controlled anger in his voice, 'because we hadn't been away more than a couple of weeks when William Craig told her he wouldn't be needing her here. I said why did she not write to tell me but, of course, I never thought to leave her with an address. We were moving around, Jeannie, in any case. She heard in the village that William Craig had made up with his father-in-law and gone back to the old man's farm, but she didn't hear anything about us coming back.' He looked at Meg. 'That would be when he knew he had to get out of here. Would you put these things away, please, Meg? Jeannie will help you. I must get out and see how my beasts are.'

'The hens are fine, and so are the cows,' Jeannie said. 'Meg and me went out to look for Glen. Daddy, does Betsy know anything about him?'

Adam shook his head.

'No, lass,' he said, and the anger had gone from his voice. 'No, Betsy doesn't know. But I will be phoning William Craig to ask him about a great many things.'

He went out the back door, and from the window Meg saw him striding across the farmyard towards the cattle-shed. With Jeannie's help, she emptied the bag of groceries and put them away. At least, she thought, we have coffee and butter and sugar and some more tins of soup.

'Real milk,' Jeannie said with pleasure. 'Thank goodness.'

The kitchen was pleasantly warm, and the water in the kettle on the Aga was ready all the time. When Adam came back Meg asked him if he would like coffee.

'In a minute, thanks. First I want to speak to William Craig. Although at least,' he said grudgingly, 'he's looked after my cattle and the hens. I'll need to get out to the fields and see the sheep.'

Jeannie had opened a packet of biscuits, and set them out.

'Betsy doesn't like us to have shop biscuits,' she told
Meg. 'I used to think it would be nice to have shop biscuits,
but I've had them while I was away and I'll be very glad
to have the things Betsy makes now. Well, not the porridge.'

Adam came back into the kitchen, and Meg handed him
a mug of coffee.

'Thanks, but I'll not sit down,' he said. 'I've a lot to do.'

He didn't look as if he wanted to talk about his phone
call, but it would have been strange not to ask, Meg
thought, so she did.

Just as Betsy had told him, Adam said, she had been
dismissed as the tenant had said he and his wife hadn't
needed her services. And the letter Adam had enclosed for
Betsy, when he'd written to say when he would be back,
was waiting at the farm for her.

'He said he didn't know where to find her,' he said,
'when all he had to do was go to the village and ask. He's
not from the glen himself, but that's no excuse.' He looked
around the kitchen. 'I think he'll have tended the animals
all right, but it doesn't look as if his wife has done much
in the house.'

Meg had been thinking that herself as she'd looked
around.

'Daddy, did you ask him about Glen?' Jeannie asked
anxiously.

Now Adam did sit down. He put his arms around the
child, and drew her close to him.

'Jeannie, lass,' he said gently, 'it seems Glen ran away,
months ago.'

What little colour there had been in Jeannie's face
drained away.

'He must have been lonely for us,' she said shakily. 'He
must have gone to see if he could find us.'

She drew back from her father's arms. 'I think I'll go to

my room for a wee while,' she said, and the heart-breaking dignity in her voice was too much for Meg.

'Oh, Jeannie,' she said, her own voice unsteady, and she would have followed the child as she went out of the kitchen but Adam's hand on her arm stopped her.

'She needs to be on her own,' he said quietly. 'She's like that when her heart is sore. We'll go to her later.' He hesitated, then he said bleakly, 'I couldn't tell her this, but something about the man's words bothered me, and I asked him right out if he'd done anything to the dog. He blustered, but then he said that the dog had needed a firm hand, and he'd had to see to that. So it looks to me as if he illtreated Glen, and that's why he ran away. He was a grand dog with the sheep, Glen, the best ever—but more than that it was what he meant to Jeannie.

'And now I'll need to be out to see the sheep. Oh—I'll go back to the village later and bring Betsy here. She'll be ready in the afternoon, she said.'

Meg went to the door with him.

'You don't need to do that today, Adam,' she said. 'You have so much to do, and now that we've got food we can manage until tomorrow.'

He looked down at her.

'Betsy must be here to stay tonight,' he said stiffly.

'But—' Meg began, but he didn't give her time to finish.

'You are not from these parts, Meg, and perhaps things are different with you. It would not be right, you and I here in the house alone.'

It was the cool dismissal in his voice, as much as the words, that made Meg so angry.

'That is so ridiculous,' she said. 'We're not alone— Jeannie is here with us.'

'Jeannie is only a child,' Adam returned curtly.

'And you are a man and I am a woman,' Meg flung back

at him. 'Does that mean we are not to be trusted to be alone together, for heaven's sake?'

He looked down at her, and his eyes were very dark.

'You are right in that, Meg,' he said quietly. 'I am a man, and you are a woman. A young woman, and a bonny one. And people would talk.'

Meg felt a slow wave of colour flood her cheeks. For the first time since she'd met him she was all at once very much aware of him as a man. Not as her employer, not as Jeannie's father, but as a tall dark man who was looking down at her with something very disturbing in his eyes.

Because of her own confusing awareness of him, she said more than she'd meant to—more than she should have, she thought later. 'Surely it doesn't matter what people say?' she said.

Now there was nothing but cool disapproval in the dark eyes, looking down at her.

'It does here in the glen,' he told her. 'And that is something you will just have to be getting used to, I'm afraid.'

CHAPTER TWO

'AND what about last night?' Meg asked, her head held high.

'That was unavoidable,' Adam replied stiffly.

Meg glared at him, at a loss for anything more to say. Suddenly, she realised how ridiculous the whole thing was, and she said so.

'Adam, this is ridiculous. Surely there is far more to think about, to worry about, than conventions?'

There was no yielding on the big man's face.

'Perhaps to you it is ridiculous,' he returned, 'but I have lived all my life here in the glen, and I will go on living here, and I will go on abiding by the ways of the glen.'

Perhaps you'll have to do that without your daughter, Meg thought. And as swiftly as it had come, her anger was gone.

'Perhaps you're right, Adam,' she said quietly. With an effort, she smiled. 'And from now on your Betsy will be here to chaperon us so we'll be all right. I'm sorry—I do tend to get on my high horse, I know that.'

She could see that he was thrown by her apology, that he didn't know quite how to handle it. She took pity on his confusion, and asked if he thought she could go and see how Jeannie was.

'She's always been a child to go off on her own when she's upset,' he said slowly. Then he went on with difficulty, 'I'm sometimes at a loss with her, Meg. I'm not sure if I'm dealing with a wee lassie the right way.'

'From what I've seen of Jeannie,' Meg said, 'I think you're doing a great job. She's a pleasant child, she's friendly, without being forward and it's been tough for her and for you, these last months.'

All the hostility had gone from his dark eyes. There was nothing there now but bleak anguish.

'And it will be even tougher,' he said, his voice low. With a determined effort to recover, he said, 'Yes, go to her. I wish I hadn't had to give her such news of Glen, but there was no kindness in keeping it from her.'

Meg went upstairs. Jeannie's door was closed, and she knocked on it.

'Jeannie? Can I come in?'

There was silence, and then Jeannie opened the door. There were tear-streaks on her face and her eyes were red, but she was composed.

'Oh, Jeannie,' Meg said. Without giving herself time to wonder if she was doing the right thing, she put her arms around the little girl. 'I'm so sorry about Glen. I can see how much he meant to you.'

'I'll find him,' Jeannie said, and Meg saw that her chin had the same determined set to it that her father's did. 'Maybe he's not far away. Maybe he's just waiting for Daddy and me to come home. I'm going to go out right now into the hills and look for him.'

'I don't think you can go right now, Jeannie,' Meg said. 'It's pouring, and it's very cold.'

Jeannie sniffed.

'A wee bit of rain never did anyone any harm,' she said.

Meg knew very well that, in spite of being in remission, Jeannie's resistance would be very low. It would be foolish to risk letting her get chilled, and Jeannie herself would have to learn to be realistic about this.

She took a deep breath.

'I would agree with you usually, Jeannie,' she said firmly, 'but you've been ill, and although you're much better now you did have to take all those pills. That does mean you have to be more careful so you can go and look for Glen on a better day.'

Jeannie's mouth was mutinous, and her grey eyes held Meg's defiantly. Meg didn't look away, and she didn't weaken, for she knew that she had to set the rules of their relationship right now.

'All right,' Jeannie said, taking her by surprise. She smiled—a shaky smile, but still a smile. 'I was right, Meg, you are bossy.'

Adam had gone on his way out to the fields when they went down, and through the rain-lashed window they could see his tall figure in an anorak, wellington boots and a cap pulled down on his dark head, striding across the farmyard to his Land Rover.

'He'll drive as far up the track as he can,' Jeannie said, 'and then he'll have to walk to where the sheep are.' She turned to Meg. 'I think I'll get my school books ready, Meg. Miss Hamilton gave me lessons to take with me, but I haven't done them all because sometimes when I was really sick I didn't feel like doing lessons. But I'll do some now because I don't want to be behind the other children. Specially Colin Cameron.

'His grandad is Betsy's brother,' Jeannie told her. 'Colin and me are the same age, and he's my best friend.' She stopped, and thought about that. 'Well, sometimes he's my best friend, but we do fight, too. And I hate it when he beats me at school. I'm better at reading and composition and things like that, but he's much better at sums.'

She went up to her room and came back with a Disneyworld backpack filled with school textbooks and exercise books. With a heavy sigh, she settled herself at one end of the big kitchen table. Meg took the chance to write to her folks as there had been no time for more than a quick phone call before she'd left the hospital.

It was dusk when Adam came back. He refused Meg's

offer to make tea, saying he had to go and collect the house-keeper right away.

He was back an hour later. By then Meg, uncertain whether she should do anything about getting a meal ready, had made tea and toast for Jeannie and herself. They'd just finished when they heard the Land Rover draw up. Jeannie ran to the door and then, suddenly shy, drew back when her father came in with a short, stout, white-haired woman.

My goodness, Meg thought, Betsy Cameron is certainly older than I thought she would be.

'Where's my wee lamb, then? And what's this nonsense? Have you not got a kiss for me, Jeannie?' the old lady demanded.

Released from her shyness, Jeannie hugged her. After a moment Betsy Cameron held the child at arm's length and studied her.

'Still a bit peely-wally,' she said severely, 'but, never mind, I'll soon have you fattened up a bit and roses in your cheeks again. It would be nothing but these hamburger things to eat in America, I suppose.'

Adam smiled, but not before Meg had seen the swift shadow in his eyes when the housekeeper spoke of roses in Jeannie's cheeks.

'You know Jeannie doesn't like "these hamburger things", Betsy,' he said mildly. 'This is Meg—Meg Bennett.'

Betsy Cameron's faded blue eyes inspected Meg from head to toe. 'Aye,' she said dismissively. 'The lassie from London.'

Meg couldn't let that pass. 'Not really from London,' she explained. 'My folks have a farm in Devon. I've been nursing in London.'

She held out her hand.

'Hello, Miss Cameron. And, please, tell me, what does—? What was the word you said—peely-something?

What does it mean?'

The housekeeper was taking her coat off.

'I'm no' accustomed to anything but Betsy—you'd better make it that,' she said grudgingly. 'And you wouldn't be knowing a good Scots word like peely-wally. Och, it just means she's a bit washed-out-looking. Jeannie Kerr, is that crumbs round your mouth and it almost teatime? Fine you know you're not supposed to be eating anything this late.'

She took an apron from her bag and tied it firmly round her ample waist.

'Now,' she said, 'I've made a stew and I just have to do some tatties. Potatoes, that is,' she told Meg. 'If you could just be peeling them, Jeannie can set the table.'

Betsy Cameron was not a woman you would argue with, Meg thought, more amused than anything else as she obediently started peeling potatoes. When the housekeeper went along to her room, off the far end of the kitchen, Adam said, 'I will tell her, Meg, that peeling potatoes isn't part of your job, or taking orders from her. I just...' He stopped.

Meg smiled. 'You just didn't feel strong enough,' she said. He looks so much younger when he smiles, she thought. 'Don't worry, Adam, I don't mind peeling potatoes or giving Betsy a hand.'

The big stove had made the kitchen warm and welcoming, but it didn't take Meg long to have her first impressions of the way the old housekeeper felt about her confirmed as anything but warm and welcoming.

After they had finished eating Adam said he would go out to see to the cattle, and also the hens, but that he would be in in time to come and say goodnight to Jeannie.

Betsy Cameron turned from the sink. 'And I suppose seeing that Jeannie gets to bed is nothing to do with me any more,' she said, with a flick of her head towards Meg. It hadn't been a question.

For a moment Adam's dark eyes met Meg's.

'Certainly, Meg is here to…take charge of Jeannie,' he said evenly. 'That's her job.'

'Daddy!' Jeannie said, and the outrage in her voice made Meg change her mind about keeping quiet. 'I don't need anyone to put me to bed.'

'Jeannie is old enough to get herself ready for bed, I think,' Meg said. 'I'll be next door, unpacking the rest of my things.'

Later, when she was setting out her make-up on the chest of drawers that would have to serve as a dressing-table, Jeannie came in her dressing-gown.

'I've run my bath, Meg,' she said, 'but, actually, I do need some help to wash my hair. I'm going to go to school tomorrow.'

I'm not so sure about that, Meg thought, but she left that for Adam to deal with. An hour later, when Jeannie's hair was dry and she was in bed, her father came out from her room.

'She says she wants to go to school tomorrow,' he said, meeting Meg in the passage.

'So why shouldn't she?' Meg replied, knowing that she sounded more belligerent than she'd meant to. She would have said more—she would have pointed out to Adam, in a matter-of-fact, sensible way, that he should let Jeannie go to school now while she was able to—but she was very conscious of Jeannie's open bedroom door, and she knew that Adam was as well.

We do have to discuss the whole thing, though, she thought, and she wondered if the same thing was in the big farmer's mind when he said, a little stiffly, that perhaps she would come and sit in the kitchen where it was warm.

'Jeannie tells me you're going to read to her before she goes to sleep,' he said. 'Come down and have a cup of tea when you've done that.'

Jeannie was sitting up in bed, her newly washed hair falling softly over her face as she opened the book she had ready.

'I can read most of it myself,' she said, a little defensively, 'but I like having it read to me.'

Meg looked at the book.

'I don't believe it,' she said, delighted. '*The Last Dragon*—one of my favourites.'

Together she and Jeannie enjoyed the story, which Meg had often read to her cousin's daughters. By the end Jeannie's eyelids were drooping. Meg kissed her lightly, and said goodnight.

'I've got my school clothes laid out,' Jeannie said sleepily. 'Daddy says you'll take me to school in the old Mini.'

Meg put out the light and went downstairs. Adam was watching the news on TV, but he turned it off when she went in.

'Betsy has gone to bed,' he told her, and Meg couldn't help feeling relieved, although an inner imp of mischief made her have to work hard to resist asking Adam if an elderly and somewhat deaf lady in her own room away along a long corridor was much of a chaperone. But the sight of the shadows in Adam's dark eyes, the tautness of his jaw, put all such thoughts in their place even before he spoke.

'You didn't say it, Meg,' he said abruptly, 'but I know you were thinking it. Jeannie may as well go to school while she can.'

He poured two mugs of tea, and handed her one.

'Tell me about her illness, Adam,' Meg said.

He told her, his voice even. Jeannie hadn't been well. Not ill, just not well. Headaches, occasional sickness, pain in her arms and legs and what she'd called 'a sore tummy'.

That, Meg knew, would be pain from an enlarged liver or spleen. To a little girl, a sore tummy.

'Go on,' she said gently.

Jeannie had always been tired, Adam said, and her face so white. The doctor had eventually said he'd wanted a blood count done.

'Dr Macrae made an appointment, and I took her to Inverness,' Adam said. He looked drained, remembering, and Meg's heart went out to him, but she had to know these things.

'I don't remember now the words they used at the hospital in Inverness,' he went on. 'Something about the white blood cells, and then they did a bone marrow test.'

'There would be an elevated white count,' Meg said quietly, and Adam agreed that that was what he had been told. By that stage, Meg knew, the peripheral blood would have shown anaemia, but the bone marrow specimen would have been diagnostic—there would have been no doubt after that.

'She had chemotherapy after that?' she asked. 'And they considered a bone-marrow transplant?'

'They did, and they said it wasn't viable,' Adam replied. 'Pills, and more pills. In Inverness, and then in Switzerland, and then in America.' His dark eyes held hers steadily. 'They told me here that they'd done all they could, you see. But I wasn't giving up. I heard about this clinic in Switzerland, and then someone there told me about this doctor in America. And now she's in remission, but no one can say how long that will last. She was longing so to come home—to the farm, to her dog. It seemed to me the best thing I could do for her.'

Afterwards, Meg's cheeks grew warm as she remembered what she'd done, immediately and instinctively. Adam's big brown hand had been resting on the table, and she'd put her own hand over it.

'Of course it was the best thing, Adam,' she said, not quite steadily, 'and there's no certainty about the prognosis.

Some children do recover. And there are new drugs, new treatments, being discovered all the time.'

His hand moved, turning to clasp hers—enclosing her hand in his. The big kitchen was all at once silent, still. So still that it took Meg a moment to realise that the uneven thudding she heard was her own heart.

Slowly Adam released her hand.

'I am not accustomed to sympathy,' he said stiffly. 'I'm sorry.'

'No, I'm sorry, I overreacted,' Meg replied, and she knew that his all too obvious withdrawal had made her do the same. Quickly—her embarrassment making her almost trip over her own words—she asked him about taking Jeannie to school.

'I started the old Mini tonight,' he told her, 'because she's always a bit difficult in winter. You did say you have a driving licence?'

He was all too relieved to be on safer ground, Meg could see, and she didn't know whether to feel amused or annoyed. Although why, she asked herself quickly, should she feel either? Adam Kerr was her employer, Jeannie's father, that was all.

She asked him, still keeping on safe ground, if he had any help on the farm.

'That's something I have to attend to tomorrow,' he said, and his lean jaw hardened. 'William Craig did more than dismiss Betsy. He brought his own folk here and told my men they weren't needed. I will have to go to the village tomorrow and see who I can find for I hear that my shepherd has left the glen. And I will have to be finding another sheepdog for I cannot do without a good dog. With a shepherd and a good dog I can get by.'

He stood.

'I go to bed early, Meg, for I rise early,' he said. 'Forgive me if I leave you now. The television set is there if you want it. Goodnight. I hope you sleep well.'

At the door he turned. 'I would like you to take Jeannie to Dr Macrae in a day or so,' he said. 'He will be keeping an eye on her.' Then, his voice carefully steady, he added, 'He is the only one in the glen who knows how serious Jeannie's illness is.'

'What about her teacher?' Meg asked.

Adam shook his head.

'Her teacher would be telling everyone she knows, and that is just about the whole glen,' he said curtly. 'Before long Jeannie would be hearing it herself, and I will not have that.'

'But Adam—' Meg began. She stood too, and he looked down at her, his eyes very dark, his lean brown face forbidding.

'Once again you must accept that you do not know how things are here in the glen,' he said abruptly. 'Goodnight.'

And goodnight to you, Adam Kerr, Meg thought, for it was too late to say it because the kitchen door had already closed behind her employer.

He can't bear to let anyone close to him, she thought, and the brief flare of anger died down. Not that I want to get close to him, or that I need to, she reminded herself, but a more friendly working relationship would certainly be easier.

With the next few days, Meg's life at Craigrannoch began to take on a pattern, a pattern that dismayed her for between the time when she took Jeannie to school and the time she picked her up in the afternoon there was nothing for her to do. She tried to talk to Adam but he was too busy organising a new shepherd, bringing in a carpenter to mend broken beams in the barn and in the cattle shed and ordering cattle fodder, to do more than tell her, a little impatiently, to use the car when she wanted to or to go out and walk.

Either alternative, Meg found, was better than trying to pass the time with Betsy Cameron's disapproving eyes on her. Her offer to peel potatoes or to prepare vegetables was met with grudging acceptance.

'Time for me to go and pick Jeannie up, and we'll be later back. I'm taking Jeannie to the doctor for a check-up,' Meg said with forced brightness one day. 'Anything you need in the village, Betsy?'

The old woman shook her head.   'I've ordered all we need,' she said, 'and the van will deliver it tomorrow morning.' She turned to stir a big pot of soup, and muttered something under her breath.

All at once Meg had had enough of this silent disapproval. 'Did you say something, Betsy?' she asked. 'I'm afraid I couldn't hear you properly.'

The housekeeper turned.

'Aye, I did,' she said. 'I said I don't know what need there is for you to be here. I've looked after Jeannie since her mother died, and before that, too.'

She didn't know, of course, Meg reminded herself, that there would at some time be a need for her as a nurse for Jeannie.

'Well, it's a help for Adam to have Jeannie's school trips done,' she said.

Betsy sniffed. An eloquent sniff, Meg thought, as she put on her warm jacket and went out to the yard.

As always, she was early for Jeannie. When the bell rang Jeannie and red-headed Colin Cameron came out, arguing fiercely about something.

Jeannie got into the car, her pale cheeks for once flushed.

'He's not my best friend any more,' she told Meg. 'He'll not come with me to look for Glen. I told him I've been out looking, and he just says I shouldn't bother. I hate him!'

Meg looked at the small red-headed boy, glaring mutinously at Jeannie. Children do quarrel, she thought, and maybe Colin has more interesting things to do than help Jeannie to look for her dog. As she leaned over to check Jeannie's seat belt the boy stepped forward.

'Jeannie,' he said, 'it's just…' He stopped.

'Just what, Colin?' Jeannie said, all too clearly very angry.

Colin Cameron scuffed his shoe on the ground.

'Nothing,' he muttered, and he turned and walked away.

Disturbed, Meg watched him. There had been something more than anger on the boy's freckled face, something she couldn't place. Pity—compassion?

Did he somehow know about the seriousness of Jeannie's illness? Or was there something else that made him feel sorry for Jeannie?

CHAPTER THREE

JEANNIE had calmed down when they reached the doctor's house, a big square stone house in the middle of the long village street. Adam had arranged for Dr Macrae to see Jeannie after surgery. When Meg and Jeannie went in, a pleasant brown-haired woman in uniform looked into the waiting-room from the doctor's office and told them Dr Macrae wouldn't be long.

A little later she came out again with a young woman, carrying a still-crying baby, his arm bandaged.

'Wee Rory pulled himself to his feet and knocked over a cup of tea,' the nurse told them when she had seen the young mother out. 'Now, Jeannie, Dr Macrae says he'll have a look at you.'

Dr Macrae was what Meg thought of as a good, old-fashioned GP, with snowy hair, bright blue eyes, a well-rounded portly figure and a kind and reassuring manner that reminded her of doctors in her childhood. When he'd examined Jeannie he patted her head.

'If you go through to the kitchen, lass, you'll see Misty's new kittens. Don't touch them for they're too young, but she'll be pleased to have you look at them.'

When Jeannie had gone he turned to Meg.

'I've seen all the reports Adam brought back,' he said quietly. 'I'm not giving up hope, by any means. As you'll know for yourself, she's fine now and in remission. There could be enough healthy elements in her bone marrow to maintain a complement of normal blood cells for some time. If not, we can have her given a transfusion.'

They talked, briefly but professionally, about what Meg

38

should keep an eye on, and Meg was pleased to find that, country doctor or not, Dr Macrae was in touch with current leukaemia research.

By the time she left him he was calling her Meg and telling her about his nephew, who was on leave from Médecins Sans Frontières and would be coming to the glen soon.

'Are you off on your rounds, then, Beth?' he asked, for the district nurse was putting on her jacket. 'Try not to be too long getting back to John.' When she'd gone he shook his head.

'Her husband has multiple sclerosis,' he said.

'He's not very great at the moment, but Beth has her rounds to do. I needed her here for surgery, too.'

He looked at her. Meg looked back at him, the same thought in both their minds.

'You were saying there's nothing for you to do, with Jeannie fine,' he said.

'I'll have to ask Adam,' Meg replied, 'but I'd be only too glad to help.' I'll ask him as soon as we get home, she decided. He should be back in by now.

However, there was another Land Rover in the farmyard. When Meg and Jeannie opened the back door and went inside, a big, burly man was standing, talking to Adam. A black and white collie lay at his feet, and Meg heard Jeannie's indrawn breath.

'Glen!' she said, and she ran across the room. Then she stopped.

'No, lass, this is Rex—he's going to be helping me with the sheep,' her father said. 'Thanks for bringing him, Gavin. I'll settle with you right now.'

Jeannie was down beside the dog, patting him.

'He's a nice dog, Mr Ferguson,' she said seriously. 'I like him fine, but I'm still going to find my Glen.'

The farmer's face darkened. He turned to Adam. 'There

is something I have to tell you. You would be hearing it sooner or later. That dog of yours—he's gone wild, and he's been killing sheep. We've all lost sheep, and we're going to catch him.'

'Are you certain that it's our Glen?' Adam asked, shock on his face.

The other man nodded.

'Aye, Adam, he's been seen beside the dead sheep, and then heading back for the foothills of Ben Vrock here on Craigrannoch. That white flash on his forehead—it's your dog, right enough. I blame William Craig. Like as not, he ill-treated the dog.'

Jeannie's small face was deathly pale, her eyes blazing, as she caught at the big farmer's arm.

'No! Glen wouldn't do that. He's trained to look after the sheep—he wouldn't hurt them!' She turned to her father. 'Daddy, tell Mr Ferguson Glen wouldn't do that—tell him!'

Adam was white, too, as he knelt and put his arms around his daughter. 'Jeannie, lass, he's been seen and recognised. We can't argue with that. I'm...deeply sorry, Gavin. You'll tell the other farmers that?'

'Aye, Adam, I'll do that.' Gavin Ferguson's voice was gruff. He looked down at Jeannie. 'You and Rex will get along fine, lass.'

'Yes, we will,' Jeannie said shakily, 'but I'll still find Glen. And—and if you do anything to hurt him I'll—'

'Jeannie,' Adam said sharply, and with one agonised look at him Jeannie ran out of the room. Meg, disregarding the command of Adam's dark brows, which were drawn together, gave him a glance of her own before she hurried out after Jeannie.

Jeannie was in her room but she wasn't crying, as Meg had expected. Her small chin was set and her eyes very bright.

'It's not true, Meg,' she said stubbornly. 'Daddy should know that. He should have told Mr Ferguson. But I know now that Glen is somewhere near, and I'll find him. I've been looking the wrong way, towards the loch, but now I know where he is. You know what, Meg? I bet Colin Cameron knows this. I bet that's why he didn't want to come with me to look for Glen.'

Meg remembered the look on the boy's face, and the impression she'd had that he was sorry for Jeannie. Yes, she thought, Jeannie was right. Colin had known about Glen.

'Jeannie, love,' she said gently as she sat down on the bed beside Jeannie, 'your daddy didn't really have any choice but to believe Mr Ferguson, and Mr Ferguson seemed to feel it was understandable that Glen had turned wild.'

'Because Mr Craig was bad to him,' Jeannie said. She shook her head. 'Glen would be lonely, and he would be sad, but he wouldn't kill sheep!'

And from that she wouldn't budge.

At Meg's insistence, she came down for tea and she apologised to her father politely. He too said that he was sorry, and he hugged her. But for the first time there was a distance between them, and Meg could see how much that hurt Adam. Later, when Jeannie was in bed and Betsy Cameron had gone to her room, she said a little awkwardly, that she had felt it was necessary to go after Jeannie.

'I could see that you didn't want me to,' she said, 'and I'm sorry about that.'

Adam sighed.

'I'm glad you did, Meg,' he said, taking her by surprise. 'She felt I had let her down—she needed someone to stand by her.' His lean dark face was bleak. 'I just hope they catch him quickly so that it's over soon, otherwise she will go on, hoping.'

I don't know what that will do to Jeannie, Meg thought, for well she knew that when Adam had said 'catch him' he'd meant 'kill him'.

Because of what had happened, she hadn't had a chance to ask Adam how he felt about her helping out with the district nurse's work, and the next morning, when she came back from taking Jeannie to school, she decided to go out to find him and talk to him.

'Which way did Adam go today, Betsy?' she asked. 'Do you know?'

'He's taken the new shepherd over to the field beside the loch,' Betsy said. 'If you're going you'd better hurry—the rain's no' far away.'

'I've got my anorak,' Meg pointed out, 'and I won't melt.'

The old housekeeper looked as if she wasn't too sure about that, but Meg ignored the disapproving look and gave Betsy a cheerful wave through the window as she hurried across the farmyard.

It was cold, and already there was rain blowing through, but Meg didn't mind that. It was good, she had to admit, to have the prospect of doing some work. She hoped Adam wouldn't mind, but surely there was no reason he should.

She could see the loch now, the water as grey and threatening as the sky above, with waves breaking on the pebbled shore. And there, beyond a stone wall—a dyke, Jeannie had called it—she could see Adam's tall figure in the middle of a flock of sheep. She called and waved, but there was no sign that he had heard her or seen her.

Close up, the sheep were bigger than she'd thought somehow. There were half a dozen of them beside the wall, grazing, and she would have to go through them to get to Adam, she realised, her heart sinking. She unlatched the gate, and carefully latched it again.

'All right, sheep, here I come,' she said aloud, more to

give herself courage than anything else. 'You stay where you are. You're close enough for my comfort, thanks.'

The sheep looked at her incuriously, and she was relieved. Except for one. The biggest one. It lifted its head, stared at her and then deliberately came towards her. Meg told herself not to panic and to walk slowly, but she found her feet had a will of their own. The faster she walked the faster the sheep came towards her. She ran towards Adam, with the large sheep gaining on her steadily.

'Adam!' she shouted.

He turned, startled.

Meg hurled herself into his arms.

'That sheep—it's chasing me,' she gasped, and now the large woolly head was butting against her. She clung to Adam, burying her head against his anorak.

After a moment she realised that although he was still holding her his whole body was shaking. She looked up at him. For the first time since she'd met him he was laughing.

'That's old Jessie—she was bottle-reared, and she still loves human company,' he told her. 'She just wants to make friends with you, Meg.'

Without letting her go, and with the laughter still on his face, he said, 'I thought you were brought up on a farm?'

Meg blushed. 'It's more a nursery, actually,' she admitted. 'My dad grows shrubs and seedlings. I just—said it. I did mean to tell you.'

'I'm sure you did,' Adam agreed gravely. 'I must say I did wonder when Jeannie said you were nervous of the cattle. And even more so the other morning when you asked who milked the cows and I had to tell you they are beef cattle.'

The tame sheep had given up and walked away.

All at once Meg was very conscious of Adam's arms around her, of his body so close to hers. He looked down at her, his eyes very dark. There was a very strange melting sensation through Meg's whole body. She knew that she should move away, but she couldn't. In fact, she thought later, her cheeks warm at the thought, perhaps she'd even moved closer to him.

Then, so abruptly that she almost lost her balance, he released her.

'The sheep will not harm you,' he said, and she wondered if she was imagining that he had to make an effort to speak evenly, 'but you would be better to walk closer to the house when the weather is so bad.'

'I wanted to ask you something,' Meg said, and she hoped that the strange and disturbing feeling had not made her voice unsteady.

She told him what Dr Macrae had said, and asked if he had any objection to her helping the district nurse, either in the surgery or on her rounds.

'I believe her husband has MS, and it's difficult for her when he has a bad turn,' she said, carefully keeping her distance now from Adam.

'Yes. John Drummond has been ill for a long time now. Beth has had a hard time.' He looked down at her. 'I don't mind, Meg, as long as it is clearly understood that when you are needed for Jeannie that is your priority.'

'So I can tell Dr Macrae that it's all right?' Meg asked. She thought quickly. 'I can drop Jeannie at school and go to the surgery then. I can do whatever I'm needed for until it's time to collect Jeannie again.'

It was a relief, she knew very well, to be able to talk about something practical like this, to be able to put from her mind that disturbing moment when Adam's arms had been around her and when she'd thought, for that one absurd moment, that he'd been going to kiss her.

Even the thought made her cheeks warm again, and she said quickly that she had better get back to the house. Adam said he would walk back with her as he had to make some phone calls.

'I'll just have a word with Jock as we pass—that's my new shepherd. I want to see how Rex is doing.'

They walked round the end of the loch, and now Meg could see another flock of sheep, with the shepherd bent over, looking at one of them.

'There are lambs due,' Adam told her, shading his eyes. 'Jock is an experienced shepherd, I was lucky to get him. Look—there's Rex, bringing in the sheep that are too far away.'

At the far end of the field she could see the collie. He was down flat, his nose on his paws, watching three sheep. Then he got up and ran towards them, expertly keeping them together and taking them to the shepherd.

'Aye, he's a good dog, right enough,' Adam said with satisfaction. But there was a shadow in his dark eyes, and his voice was low. 'And so was Glen—the best sheepdog I've ever had. Wait here, Meg, I'll only be a minute.'

She watched him stride across the field, and she thought how completely at home he looked here. The brief meetings in London... She realised now that he had been out of place, a little uncomfortable. Here, in the glen, with the sheep around him, the dog at his feet—even the stormy water of the loch and the threatening clouds—seemed the right place for this man.

On the way back to the house, he asked her about her father's nursery, and she thought that he, too, was glad to be on safe ground.

Then, with the house in sight, he said, a little awkwardly, 'You said something about being jilted, and wanting to get away. I'm not wanting to pry at all, but I just wanted to say I'm sorry.'

It surprised Meg how seldom she'd thought of Simon, since she'd come to the farm.

'I thought my heart was broken,' she said lightly, 'but I think now it was more my pride that was hurt. And getting away from the hospital was the best thing I could have done.'

'He must have been a fool,' Adam said, and Meg didn't know how to reply to that. They had just turned into the farmyard, and there was a blue sports car parked beside the Land Rover.

'Oh, Helen's here,' Adam said, opening the kitchen door.

Betsy Cameron was sitting at the big kitchen table, looking considerably more cordial than Meg had yet seen her, with a young woman beside her. A very elegant young woman, Meg thought, with shining blonde hair falling, smoothly to her shoulders, and perfect make-up, the green of her eyeshadow matching the tailored corduroy trousers she wore. A sheepskin-lined jacket was flung casually over the back of a chair. Meg was all too conscious of her unruly brown curls, her unadorned face and her well-worn jeans.

'Adam, my dear.'

Meg stood while Adam was greeted with a kiss. I feel, she thought, like a spare part. I don't know whether to move away or to wait.

'Helen, this is Meg Bennett,' Adam said. 'Meg—Helen Ferguson. It's Helen's father who let me have Rex. Are you home for long, Helen?'

Long, slim fingers touched Meg's hand for a moment in greeting, and the slim shoulders shrugged.

'A few days this time—I've got a good assistant, and I needed a break.'

'Helen has an antique shop in Inverness,' Adam explained.

Betsy had poured coffee for Adam and Meg, but Adam didn't sit down, explaining that he had to make some phone calls. Helen Ferguson put one hand on his arm.

'I'm so glad you and Jeannie are back, Adam,' she said,

'and that Jeannie is so much better. These glandular fever things can take a long time, I believe.'

For a moment Adam's eyes met Meg's. Yes, she thought, an acceptable explanation of Jeannie's illness. But he said nothing more, and went off to make his phone calls.

Helen Ferguson finished her coffee.

'Thanks, Betsy, that was good,' she said. Her eyes, grey and cool, studied Meg. 'I'm surprised that Adam feels he needs someone to look after Jeannie,' she said. Betsy Cameron had taken the mugs over to the sink, and Helen glanced at the old housekeeper's broad back before she lowered her voice a little. 'Although, I suppose, Jeannie not having a mother, he thought it would be a good idea to have someone young around until...'

She paused.

Until what? Meg thought, but she was darned if she was going to respond. She said nothing, and after a moment Helen said she must be going and put her jacket on.

'Bye, Betsy,' she said. 'See you soon.' After a slight hesitation she added, 'Bye Meg. Don't let the glen get you down. It must be quite a change for you, coming away from the city lights.' A moment or two later there was the powerful sound of her car, driving off up the farm road.

Meg, hanging up her anorak, turned to find Betsy Cameron's eyes on her.

'I'm sure we will be seeing Helen soon,' the old housekeeper said with satisfaction. 'She and Adam are good friends. Although she lives in Inverness, she belongs to the glen.'

And I don't, Meg thought.

Then she lifted her chin. Why on earth should that bother me? I'm here to do a job, that's all. The job of looking after Jeannie if and when her remission ended and she was ill again.

The sobering thought of that was far more important than anything Betsy Cameron or Helen Ferguson could say.

'Then I'll go by myself,' Jeannie said.

The mutinous set of her chin was becoming familiar to Meg. She had to maintain her authority and take a stand on some things, but perhaps this need not be one of them.

'All right, I'll come with you,' she said, when the intensity of Jeannie's grey eyes was more than she could take. 'But just suppose we do find your Glen—and I don't for a moment think we will—what are you going to do, Jeannie?'

Jeannie looked away, but not before Meg had seen the defiance fade, leaving her small face so vulnerable that Meg's heart ached for her.

'I don't know,' she admitted, not quite steadily, 'but I have to look for him, Meg.'

'Right, then,' Meg said with determined briskness. 'Let's get ready for that cold wind outside. Is it going to rain, do you think?'

Jeannie glanced out the kitchen window.

'No, because you can still see the path as far as the loch,' she said. 'If you can't see it that far, it's going to rain, Daddy says.'

'And if you can't see it any further than the farmyard, it's already raining,' Meg returned.

They were just going out the back door when Betsy came through from the pantry.

'And where are you going, and that east wind so snell?' she demanded.

'Just out for a walk, Betsy,' Jeannie said airily. 'You always say fresh air is good for people.'

The old housekeeper tucked in Jeannie's scarf. 'Aye, well, you're well enough wrapped up,' she admitted grudgingly.

Meg and Jeannie set off along the path towards the gorse-covered hillside, Jeannie explaining that 'snell' meant the wind was cold and biting into you.

'But we can't just wait for the weather to get better, Meg,' she said seriously. 'There's no chance to get out on a school day because it's almost dark when we get home so we have to go today. And tomorrow.'

Her small mittened hand crept into Meg's.

'Can you whistle, Meg?' she asked. 'Glen might hear a whistle better than me calling.'

Meg demonstrated her ability to whistle, and after a few tries to get the sound right Jeannie was satisfied. She looked around her.

'There are caves further up,' she said, 'but some of the path is a bit steep. We can try here.'

For half an hour Meg whistled and Jeannie called.

'I think we'll have to leave it for now, Jeannie,' Meg said. 'You're cold, I can see.'

'I'm not cold,' Jeannie replied, but her small face was pinched. 'Can't we go just a little further, Meg?'

Meg shook her head.

'Not today,' she said. 'If we can, we'll come out again tomorrow.'

She took Jeannie's hand in hers, and after a moment she could see that she wasn't going to argue. They turned back onto the path down to the farmhouse.

'Tell me about Glen when he was a puppy, Jeannie,' Meg said, and Jeannie's face lit up.

'He was so little, Meg,' she said. 'And he was so lonely for his mother the first few nights, but Daddy put a stone hot-water bottle wrapped in a blanket and an alarm clock in his bed, and then he settled. He missed the other puppies, you see, and he missed his mother.' Then, with a matter-of-fact acceptance that made Meg's throat tight, she said, 'I knew how he was feeling because it wasn't long after Mummy died, and I still missed her.'

Meg hesitated, but only for a moment.

'Do you remember your mother, Jeannie?' she asked gently.

'I'm not sure,' Jeannie said, her voice low. 'Sometimes I think I remember things, like Mummy bathing me and wrapping me in a big towel and kissing me goodnight when I was in bed, but—but sometimes I think I just like thinking I remember. I was only three, you see, and that's not very old.'

'No, Jeannie, it isn't,' Meg agreed.

'Before I was ill I used to go to Colin's house after school sometimes,' Jeannie said then. 'Colin's quite naughty, and sometimes his mother used to be very angry with him. Do you know, Meg, I used to think it must be so nice even to have your mother being angry with you. Just—just having your mother there.'

They'd reached the farmyard and already, although it was only early afternoon, there was a welcoming light shining from the kitchen window.

'Betsy might have hot chocolate ready for us,' Jeannie said. At the door she looked up at Meg. 'Betsy's very good at looking after me. And Daddy and I do a lot of things together, but daddies are different, aren't they?'

Meg agreed that daddies were different as she followed Jeannie into the kitchen.

There was no chance to look for Glen the next day because it was raining. Without the matter being discussed, neither Jeannie nor Meg mentioned to Adam that they'd gone out looking for him.

On Monday morning, after she had dropped Jeannie at school, Meg went to the surgery. She had phoned Dr Macrae to tell him that she would be coming in, and they had agreed that the district nurse, Beth Drummond, would work with her at least for the first surgery time.

It was a strange feeling, being in uniform again and yet not in hospital, Meg thought as Beth showed her the patients' files.

'This is all very different from working in a hospital,' she said a little doubtfully, glancing at the waiting patients.

'You'll do fine, Meg,' the older woman said reassuringly. 'Right, I'm going to change this dressing first, and Dr Macrae will have a look at the wound.'

Expertly, she took the old dressing off a red-haired man's foot, and Meg saw that the gash—a nasty one—was clean and free of infection.

'Aye, Harry, you'll be more careful with a pitchfork after this, I'm thinking,' the old doctor said. 'Fine, Nurse, you can put a new dressing on. Come back on Friday, Harry, and we'll change the dressing again.'

There were prescriptions to be renewed—one for low blood pressure, another for a duodenal ulcer. Then there was a small child to have her tonsils checked, three flu patients and a woman with diabetes to have her insulin level checked. After the surgery was clear Meg went with the district nurse on her rounds.

There were two patients to be bathed, a new mother and her baby to be seen and an old man who had had a hip replacement.

'I'll have to get all their names straight,' Meg said. 'That was Mrs Campbell with the new baby?'

Beth Drummond nodded.

'Ailie Campbell, and wee Morag,' she said. 'You'll get to know them, Meg. Look, would you mind if we looked in at my own house to see how John is?'

Before she started the car she told Meg, her voice level and steady, that her husband had been diagnosed with multiple sclerosis five years previously.

'You know the course of it yourself,' she said quietly. 'It was some time before we got the diagnosis, but there was the slurred speech first of all, and then he had attacks of vertigo and trouble with his hands and his feet.'

'Spastic weakness of the extremities,' Meg said, remembering the wording in her nursing manual.

The older woman nodded.

'I wonder, now, why I didn't see earlier for myself because I've nursed a few MS patients. But I suppose it might have been a denial thing. I just didn't want to admit the possibility.'

'How is he now?' Meg asked.

'You know how it is,' Beth Drummond said. 'The symptoms come and go with increased frequency and severity. He's on ACTH when there's an acute attack. Right now he isn't too bad. He can still walk around the house. So we're making the most of that.'

Until next time, Meg thought. She too had nursed a few MS patients, and she knew the picture well. She also knew what had to be done at that stage.

'I know rehabilitation measures won't alter the disease process,' she said, 'but if you can try for functional improvement…'

The district nurse's brown eyes were shadowed.

'He's had physio when he's been in hospital, but the glen is too far away and too small for us to have a physiotherapist here. I do try to help him to do daily exercises to combat the muscle dysfunction,' she said, 'but sometimes I'm late home, and by then John is tired. He has a contract job with a computer company and, for more reasons than the money, I want him to keep on with that as long as possible.'

I don't want to push in where I'm not wanted, Meg thought. But at the same time… 'I've worked on an orthopaedic ward, and that's where we had a couple of MS patients. They'd both had limbs splinted, and they had daily physio. I have a little experience—I can think of a couple

of things right away. We did a stretch, hold, relax routine
that was very helpful in treating muscle spasticity. Maybe
I could look in whenever possible, and do what I can. What
do you think?'

It was a moment before the older woman replied.

'I think that would be wonderful,' she said, not quite
steadily. 'It would mean that John could have exercise
when he's fresh enough to benefit from it.'

She started the engine, drove to the top end of the village
and stopped outside a small stone cottage with a small but
pretty garden.

'John's always been keen on his garden,' she said, as she
opened the front gate. 'He can't do much now, though.'

John Drummond was sitting at his computer and, without
turning, he said,   'I'll just save this, Beth. I've got a good
lot done today.'

Beth waited a moment until he turned. She introduced
Meg to him, and he came across the room awkwardly, leaning on two sticks and balancing on one as he shook her
hand. His wife told him what she and Meg had been dis-
cussing, and he agreed, with a reserve which was all too
plain to Meg, that it would be a help to Beth.

'And to you, John,' Beth pointed out, but he didn't reply
to that. She made tea, and she and Meg had theirs quickly,
leaving her husband's on a tray beside him.

'He's very independent,' the district nurse said defensively as she closed the gate again. 'He hates it that he
needs help. When the bairns are home at the weekend he'll
hardly even accept an offer from them to make a cup of
tea.'

Their children, she told Meg, were at high school in
Inverness, staying with a cousin of Beth's. Talking of
school reminded Meg to mention that she would always
have to be finished in time to meet Jeannie and take her
home.

It worked well, she found, as that first week went by. Gradually she found herself becoming more confident both with helping the old doctor in surgery and with accompanying Beth Drummond as she did her rounds. Most days she managed to fit in half an hour with John Drummond, doing exercises with him, and she hoped that there was a cautious beginning of acceptance there. By the end of the week she was doing some visits on her own, and beginning to sort out the names of her patients.

'You're enjoying this work, I see, Meg,' Adam said one night, when she came downstairs after they had both said goodnight to Jeannie. 'I caught a glimpse of you coming out of old Hector Gray's house the other day, and you looked very professional and businesslike.'

'Yes, I'm enjoying it,' Meg replied. 'It fits in well with the school times, and Beth knows I must finish in time to collect Jeannie from school.'

'I'm glad this came up for you,' Adam said abruptly. 'It must have been pretty boring for you, all that time on your own. And just a wee lassie for company after that. I'm afraid there's a lot I have to catch up with in the bookwork and the accounts for the farm. Things are in a bit of a mess. And I'm afraid that I'm off back to the office again to do some work. I'm not much company either. I'll be out tomorrow night. Gavin and Mary Ferguson have asked me to go and have a bite to eat with them.'

And, of course, their glamorous daughter, Meg thought.

For a moment, his dark eyes met hers. She had the uncomfortable feeling that he knew what she was thinking.

'You'd better go and do your work, then,' she said lightly, 'so that you'll be free tomorrow night.' She bent and patted the dog, who had got into the habit of lying at her feet. 'Rex and I enjoy sitting here together.'

Adam patted the dog, too, and the silky black tail, white-tipped, wagged. 'He's a good dog, aren't you, Rex?' he said.

As he reached the door, he stopped. 'I hope you're not sorry you came, Meg,' he said. 'I didn't mislead you. I did tell you that you might not be needed for a while.'

Meg went over to him. 'And I hope I'm not—for a very long time, if at all,' she said.

The lines of the big man's face tightened.

'Every day I look at her,' he said, his voice low, 'and I say to myself that just for today she's fine, so make the most of that.'

He looked down at her.

'She's a serious wee lass, my Jeannie,' he said. 'But since you came here with us I've heard her laugh, and I've seen her smile more than she has for a long time. I'm— grateful for that, Meg.'

For one moment Meg had the most ridiculous and foolish urge to stand on tiptoe and kiss this big, quiet man. Just a quick, comforting kiss on the cheek. She wondered what he'd do if she did—what he'd do if he even knew she'd thought of it. If nothing else, the disturbing memory of how she had felt in his arms, in the field beside the loch, would have stopped her.

'I'm very fond of Jeannie, Adam,' she said, meaning it. 'I enjoy her company, and I have no regrets.' Then, unable to resist the impulse, she said demurely, 'But Rex and I enjoy your company, too, when we have the chance of it.'

For a moment she thought she'd gone too far, and then Adam burst out laughing.

'I can take a hint,' he said. 'What about the four of us— you and I, and Jeannie and Rex—having a wee run to the sea at the weekend? Would you like that? Good. And now I really am off to do some work.'

When he'd gone Meg sat by the fire, her book on her lap, thinking how much younger Adam looked when the darkness left his face. It would be better for Jeannie, as well as for himself, if he could just...lighten up a bit. Hard to do, she understood that very well, but, yes, better for Jeannie.

But I don't know, she thought, if I could say that to him. There was no doubt that there was less strain, less tension, between them. She hoped that any doubts he'd had about the wisdom of employing her, in spite of her youth, had gone. It certainly seemed so, from what he'd said about being grateful to her because of Jeannie laughing, but she still felt there was reservation, a barrier, and if she got too close to that barrier she could be in trouble.

Whatever, she told herself, it was a relief to be on more friendly terms with her boss. And it would be lovely to go to the sea at the weekend.

She'd told Dr Macrae and Beth Drummond that she wouldn't be able to help on Saturdays, that she'd be with Jeannie then. She knew very well what was in Jeannie's mind when Saturday morning was clear and bright, with a cold March wind blowing and white clouds scudding in the pale blue of the sky.

'Can't we go out right now, Meg?' Jeannie said impatiently.

'As soon as I've finished my ironing, Jeannie,' Meg promised. 'I have to have my uniforms ready for Monday, and your daddy said we might have a run to the sea so I'd better get this done now.'

'Daddy's gone to the village to send some registered letter to the lawyer about that man who was supposed to look after the farm. He won't be back for ages 'cos he'll have to wait for Betsy to finish the shopping,' Jeannie said. 'So we won't be going out till afternoon or maybe even tomorrow.'

'I'll be ready in ten minutes,' Meg said firmly.

Jeannie heaved a deep sigh, but a few minutes later she

appeared with her anorak on and a large basket in her hand, saying she would go and collect eggs. 'That will be a help to Betsy,' she said. 'No, Rex, you stay with Meg.'

It didn't occur to Meg to wonder why Jeannie didn't want Rex to come out with her, and it was only later that she remembered the guileless look in Jeannie's grey eyes.

She had almost finished her ironing when there was a phone call for Adam, and by the time she'd written down the details of the message, and taken the number for him to call back, she heard the Land Rover draw up at the back door.

Adam came in, taking off his warm jacket as he came.

'I'll go back for Betsy later,' he said. 'It was a good chance for her to have a wee while with her sister. Hello, boy,' he said, ruffling Rex's silky ears as the dog greeted him, his tail wagging.

He looked around. 'Where's Jeannie?'

Collecting eggs, Meg told him. Adam frowned, and said it was strange that she hadn't come out from the barn when she'd heard him come.

Meg's heart plummeted. She knew exactly where Jeannie had gone. She took a deep breath, but there was no easy way to get round this.

'I think she's gone to look for Glen,' she said baldly.

The big farmer's face went very still, the line of his jaw hard and unrelenting as he strode across the kitchen to her.

'And just why do you think that?' he asked, his voice harsh.

Meg told him that she and Jeannie had been out before, that Jeannie wanted to go again this morning and—this with difficulty, under the anger in Adam's dark eyes—that she had promised to go out again with Jeannie as soon as she had finished ironing.

'You were deliberately defying my wishes—you know

that,' Adam said tightly. He zipped up his jacket again. 'Do you know which way she would go?'

'She spoke about caves in the foothills,' Meg told him. She switched off the iron, and lifted her own jacket from its peg.

'I'm coming too,' she said, but he didn't even acknowledge that as he strode out, whistling to the collie as he went. Meg hurried after him, breathless by the time she caught up with him on the path she and Jeannie had followed a few days previously.

After some time she ventured to speak. 'She won't come to any harm,' she said. 'And she can't have been gone long—we'll catch up with her.'

Without looking at her, he strode on.

'There's been more sheep-killing,' he said. 'Gavin Ferguson told me the other night that the dog was seen again, making in this direction. The farmers are determined to catch him. They could be out with guns right now, heading for the very place you say Jeannie would be going to.'

Jeannie had on her scarlet anorak, and would be easily seen. Meg wanted to say so but before she could there was a bark from Rex, and there, running down the path towards them, was Jeannie.

Adam and Meg ran towards her. The child's cheeks were flushed, her eyes bright.

'I saw him, Daddy, I saw Glen,' she called, before she reached them. 'He ran away, but I know it was him.'

They met, and Meg looked anxiously at Jeannie, breathless after running to them. But she seemed to be all right—in fact, Meg thought, with a wave of relief, right now she looked like a normal, healthy child.

'He wouldn't come to me,' Jeannie said sadly, 'but he will next time, I know he will.'

'Jeannie,' her father said. His face was like thunder as he looked down at his small daughter. 'There will be no next time,' he said. 'You are not to go looking for the dog again. He has been seen, killing more sheep.'

CHAPTER FOUR

ALL the colour drained from Jeannie's face.

She shook her head. 'No,' she whispered, 'it isn't true, Daddy—it can't be. You know Glen wouldn't do that.'

Adam's anger had gone. He knelt on the path, and put his arms around his small daughter.

'Jeannie, lass, he's been seen, and he's been recognised. And...' he hesitated '...they are out now, looking for him. We'd best go home.'

He stood up and held out his hand, but Jeannie didn't take it. She walked ahead of Adam and Meg, her fair head bent. Fighting back tears, Meg thought, and her heart ached for the child. But one involuntary step towards the sad little figure, and the look on Adam's face, told her that while he could not go on being angry with Jeannie there was no doubt that he was still angry with her. Very angry.

Without waiting for them, Jeannie opened the back door and went into the house. Adam stopped and looked down at Meg.

'It was wrong, and it was irresponsible to encourage her in this foolishness,' he said, and the controlled steadiness of his voice, the cold fury in his dark eyes, made it difficult for Meg to stand her ground, to hold her head high.

'I didn't know there were men out after the dog,' she said. 'If I'd known that of course I wouldn't have agreed to go with Jeannie.'

It didn't seem wise to remind him that in any case Jeannie had gone without her although, to be fair, when she thought of Jeannie's refusal to take Rex with her, and the guileless look in her eyes, she should perhaps have been suspicious.

Jeannie's father was well aware of this, she realised.

'You are in charge of Jeannie,' he said brusquely, 'and that means being aware of what is in her mind to do.' Then, disconcertingly, his anger was gone. 'Meg, there will be nothing but heartbreak for Jeannie if she is allowed to think she can find the dog and win him back.'

'What is she facing now but heartbreak, Adam?' Meg asked, not quite steadily.

However, he was right, she knew. Yet the way Jeannie had looked, the joy on her face as she'd run towards them—it was hard to take that away from her.

Adam didn't reply and he didn't ask her to make any promises. Meg was to remind herself of that later.

Jeannie was quiet and subdued for the rest of that day. She wasn't sulking—Meg had already found that Jeannie was not a child to sulk—just low in spirits, Meg thought, remembering her grandmother saying that about someone.

The thought of her own grandmother, and how dear and secure a part of her own childhood she had been—and still was—made Meg ask Adam that evening, after Jeannie was in bed, if there were no grandparents. He shook his head, and told her that his wife's parents had died when she was a child, and his own mother and then his father when Jeannie was a baby.

'Remiss of me, not to have grandparents for Jeannie,' he said a little awkwardly, and she could see that he was trying to bridge the gap between them.

The next morning, when the weather was once again fine, he suggested that they might take a picnic and drive over to the sea.

'Would you like that, Jeannie?' he said.

'Yes, thank you, Daddy, that would be very nice,' Jeannie said politely.

And politeness is all you'll get, I'm afraid, Meg thought, seeing the disappointment on Adam's face.

Jeannie did brighten up a little, though, when they drove out of the glen, over the bridge and through a narrow road leading between rugged hills.

'We're nearly there,' Jeannie said, leaning forward. 'You'd hardly think we were so close to the sea, would you, Meg?'

Meg agreed that she certainly wouldn't think so as the road suddenly came out of the hills, and the sea was before them. The road, such as it was, became no more than a rough track, and soon Adam drew up before the rough grass ended and the silver sands swept down to a small bay.

'Button up your anorak, you will find it's always colder here at the sea,' Adam said, as Meg climbed down. 'Jeannie, put your gloves on.'

Jeannie walked sedately to the edge of the grass, the collie at her heels. There were seagulls on the wet sands, and the dog ran towards them. After a moment Jeannie ran down on to the shore as well.

'Jeannie—take your time,' her father called, but the wind was strong and his words had no chance of reaching the small girl and the black and white dog. He looked down at Meg. 'She should not be using up her strength running, surely,' he said, anxiously.

'Give her a little while, Adam,' Meg said, watching the child and the dog. 'A little running won't do her any harm.'

In a few minutes Jeannie slowed down, walking along the wet sand, while the dog ran hopefully after the swooping seagulls.

They caught up with her, and already some of the reserve she had been showing to her father was gone, Meg was glad to see. Sometimes, though, there was a shadow on Jeannie's face when Rex barked excitedly or when he found a piece of seaweed and dragged it along the sand. It was all too clear to Meg and, she was sure, to Adam that Jeannie was thinking of her own dog. I suppose they used to come here with him, too, she thought, and Jeannie's words confirmed that.

'Rex is enjoying this,' Adam said, as they turned back. 'He'll be thinking this is a better thing than working in the fields.'

'Dogs always like coming to the beach,' Jeannie said, and although her voice was matter-of-fact her grey eyes were very bright. Too bright, Meg thought, her heart going out to the little girl.

She bent and picked up a shell, and held it out to Jeannie.

'Just for a minute I thought it was a pansy shell,' she said. 'Do you get pansy shells here?'

'I've never found one,' Jeannie said, 'but Colin Cameron's daddy found one, and he gave it to Colin's mummy, and she still has it. I've seen it.' She hesitated, and looked up at her father. 'I'm glad Rex likes the beach, Daddy,' she said, and Meg and Adam could see that she, too, was doing her best to bridge the gap.

Later they found a sheltered place to have the picnic Betsy had got ready for them. Cold chicken, rolls and hot coffee had never tasted as good, Meg thought.

'Look,' Jeannie said suddenly, excitement in her voice. 'Seals—over there, at the far side of the bay.'

Sure enough, there were half a dozen sleek black heads beside the black rocks.

'Will they come any further in?' Meg asked, and she smiled at herself for talking softly. The seals were far away, and the sound of the sea, pounding on the shore, would have hidden any sound.

'I doubt it,' Adam said, shaking his head. 'They're shy creatures, seals.'

Jeannie looked up at her father.

'Maybe they're not seals at all,' she said softly. Maybe

they're silkies. Oh—I don't suppose you'll know about the silkies, Meg, you being English,' she said.

'The silkies?' Meg repeated. 'No, I don't. What are they?'

Jeannie moved closer to her father. 'The silkies are seal-women. Tell Meg about them, Daddy,' she said.

Adam smiled.

'It's a long story so we'd better be sitting down. Well, now, we'll have to start with the seals,' he said. 'They say the seals are the children of the King of Lochlann, and a wicked stepmother put a spell on them. I've heard it said that you can tell by the very eyes of the seals that there is royal blood in them. The silkies, now, are seal-women.'

Jeannie's eyes were on her father's face. Meg, listening, thought that the sound of Adam's voice, deep and dark, with the Highland lilt in it, gave the story an irresistible magic.

'They say, in the Highlands and the islands, that some-times a man will be finding a seal-woman bathing in the creek, and she without her sealskin. If he finds it, and if he hides it, then on the third night he can marry her. But if ever she finds the sealskin that was hers—and they say it is softer than mist to the touch—then he will lose her, for she will take it, and she will go back to the cool sea-water that she has been longing for all the years she has lived with him. And when she gets there she will sing her sea-joy. And all he will have is the sound of her singing, and the memory of her, for all the rest of his life.'

Meg felt the sting of tears behind her eyes.

'It's a lovely story, Adam,' she said, not quite steadily, 'but so sad.'

Adam's dark eyes held hers, and there was something disturbing and troubling in his look.

'Yes,' he agreed, 'it is a sad story. But surely a man should have more sense than to keep a seal-woman away from the sea, to keep her in a place that is not meant for her?'

It's only a story, Meg told herself. He doesn't mean me to take anything out of it. It's just his way of—of finishing off the story.

'I thought you would like hearing about the silkies, Meg,' Jeannie said with satisfaction. She stood up. 'I think I'll take Rex for a wee walk. We won't go really close to the seals, but just where we can get a better view.' With an oddly grown-up air she added, 'I'll go by myself.'

Meg and Adam watched her walk along the silver sand, sedately at first but with an occasional little skip that removed some of Meg's concern for her.

'She's what my grandmother would call an old-fashioned little thing,' Meg said, as she finished clearing up the picnic things.

'Yes, she is,' Adam agreed. 'She's been too much with grown-ups this last few months. She needs to remember that she's just a wee lassie. She was asking if Colin Cameron could come and play after school sometimes. Would you mind bringing him back with Jeannie some days, Meg?'

'I'd be very pleased to,' Meg said. Feeling for the right words, she said carefully, 'We need to treat Jeannie as a normal child as far as possible, Adam.'

He nodded.

'I know—and I know, too, that you are telling me I am over-protective of her. It is hard not to be, but a laddie like Colin to play with will do her the world of good.'

Far along the beach Jeannie was sitting on a rock, with the collie beside her. Meg lay down on the travelling-rug, enjoying the faint warmth of the late winter sunshine on her face. She closed her eyes, and in her mind she could hear again Adam's deep voice, telling the story of the silkies.

'Have a sleep if you want to, Meg,' he said softly.

Meg opened her eyes, startled to find how close to her he was, leaning on one elbow and looking down at her.

She started to say that she wasn't sleepy, that she had just closed her eyes, but something in the dark stillness of his face silenced her. That, and his closeness to her. She could hear the sea, surging in to the shore, and now she could hear the uneven thudding of her own heart.

I should move away, she thought. I should do something—say something.

But she knew very well that the last thing in the world she wanted to do was to move away from this man. Gently, his lips touched hers. Gently, softly—and then not at all gently, with an urgent demand that found an immediate response in her whole body.

Slowly he released her, and she could see that he was as shaken as she was. He sat up, and so did she.

'I don't know what to say,' Adam said at last. 'I should not have done that, Meg, and I apologise. It would be best if we could both be forgetting that it happened.'

Afterwards, Meg wondered if there might have been a better way of responding, but the wave of confusion and disappointment that swept through her made her lift her chin, reply lightly, casually, 'For goodness' sake,' she said, 'it was only a kiss.'

Only a kiss? Her own words resonated in her with a sense of betrayal for she knew all too well that no other kiss in all her life had made her feel the way she had just then in Adam's arms. But she was darned if she would let him know that after what he had just said.

For a moment longer his dark eyes held hers, then he turned away.

'You are right,' he said, his voice as light and as casual as her own. 'It was only a kiss.'

He stood.

'Here is Jeannie, coming back,' he said. 'We should be going home now—there is a sea-mist out there and the cold will come in from the sea.'

Fortunately, Meg thought, it didn't take them long to drive back to the farm. Jeannie was quiet, clearly a little tired, and she herself found it hard to make polite conversation with Adam. It was a relief when he went off soon after Jeannie went to bed—to visit Gavin Ferguson, he said.

I suppose it would be because of Helen Ferguson that he said he shouldn't have kissed me, Meg couldn't help thinking. Well, I suppose he's right. Even without Helen Ferguson, this is a working relationship and it shouldn't be—obscured—by anything else.

She was in bed when she heard the Land Rover pull up outside the farmhouse, and she was taken aback to have to admit to a small shock of pleasure at the realisation that Adam hadn't, in fact, stayed at the Fergusons for long.

The only reference he made to his visit was a low comment to Meg, when Jeannie ran upstairs after breakfast next morning to get her school books.

'They didn't catch the dog,' he said abruptly. 'Gavin Ferguson and some of the other farmers went out looking for him, but they couldn't find him.'

There was no chance for him to say anything further as Jeannie came back into the kitchen.

'Do I have to have porridge, Daddy?' Jeannie asked, sitting at the table. 'Can't I have muesli, like Meg does?'

Meg had been delighted to find her favourite muesli in the village shop. Although every morning she was very conscious of Betsy Cameron's disapproval, she went to the pantry herself and brought it out at breakfast-time.

'She'd be getting oats in a different form, Adam,' she pointed out. 'And other things that are good for her.'

Jeannie smiled.

'And I like it so I'd eat more of it,' she said.

Neither Jeannie nor Meg, with their backs to the door, had realised that the old housekeeper had come in. Now, with a glare at Meg, she whisked away the plate of porridge set at Jeannie's place.

'Fine, then,' she threw over her shoulder, 'I'll just give this to the dog, and from now on it's be porridge for you and me, Adam, and Jeannie can have that fancy stuff. Here, Rex.' She went off, muttering something about all these years and fancy nonsense.

'I'm sorry, Adam,' Meg said, dismayed.

'It's all right,' Adam replied. 'You're quite right—enjoy your muesli, Jeannie. Betsy will get over it.' He smiled. 'I like it myself—had it quite often when we were away, didn't I, Jeannie?'

He stood, whistled for Rex and said it was time he was off.

'It's all right for Colin to come back with me to play?' Jeannie asked, and her father nodded.

Betsy's disapproval was still very evident when Meg and Jeannie left.

'I didn't realise she would be so annoyed,' Meg said.

'She always sort of huffs and puffs when she's angry,' Jeannie said, and Meg agreed that she had noticed that.

'Like the wolf in the "Three Little Pigs",' Jeannie said, as Meg drew up at the school gate. 'There's Colin—see you later, Meg.'

Meg watched the little girl run across the school playground to meet the red-headed boy, waiting for her. She looks all right, she thought as she did every day, trying unobtrusively to check her charge. Adam did the same, she knew, his dark eyes on his daughter with an anxiety he tried to hide. For now she's fine, Meg told herself, and she drove off to the surgery.

'A full waiting-room, I see,' she said to Beth Drummond, and the district nurse nodded.

'It's the changing season,' she said. 'We always get fluey and chesty things.' She handed Meg a list. 'Would you mind checking on these folks? I think I'll be more use here in the surgery today.'

Meg took the list, and Beth's bag, and set off. She was finding that she really enjoyed doing the rounds, getting to know some of the village people.

Her first call was to change the dressing for the toddler whose arm had been burned.

'I would have brought him to the surgery, Nurse,' his mother apologised, 'but I've got this awful cold myself, and Dr Macrae says he doesn't want me out in this wind after the bronchitis I had a wee while ago.'

'Very wise, too,' Meg said. 'Right, Rory, let's have a look at your arm.'

The little boy looked back at her, his lower lip jutting out.

'No, Nursie,' he said, very definitely.

'Yes, Rory,' Meg replied, just as definitely. 'Tell you what, we'll put a nice new bandage on your arm, and then we'll put one on Teddy.'

The burn was healing nicely, and she cleaned off some of the dead skin, before dressing the small arm and putting on a new bandage. Then, carefully, she put a small bandage on the teddy's arms.

'Make Teddy better,' Rory said, and she agreed that it would make Teddy better.

Still smiling at this, she went on up the road to do a bed-bath for old Mrs Hamilton, who'd had a hip replacement. Then she checked on a diabetes patient, and after that made a visit to an old couple, Mr and Mrs Gow, the old man recovering from pleurisy and the old lady crippled with arthritis.

'I think we'll ask Dr Macrae to look in later and check

your chest, Mr Gow,' she said, and made a note about that, not happy about the old man's breathing.

There was time for a quick visit to John Drummond, before going back to the surgery. She knocked at the back door and opened it.

'It's me, John,' she called, and she went through to the room where he worked on his computer.

There was almost, she thought, a smile of welcome from Beth's husband. He had been very suspicious of Meg's visits at first, and had even said that he thought it was a waste of time. But now he moved awkwardly from his seat at the computer over to the couch.

'And what is it you said you're doing now?' he asked, as Meg gently worked on his arms.

'Progressive resistance exercises,' Meg told him. 'To strengthen weak muscles.'

John Drummond's blue eyes held hers.

'Your exercises will not give me back the strength I once had, though, Meg,' he said, and it wasn't a question.

'No, John, I'm afraid not,' Meg replied, 'but we're going to do all we can to hold it at this level.' For as long as possible, she thought, and she knew that John Drummond was thinking the same.

'Aye, we'll go down fighting,' he said, and she thought, as she drove back to the surgery, that this was a move for the better—to have him talking like that.

Surgery over, she thought as she parked her car. Maybe Beth will need me to look in on some more folks.

'I'm back, Beth,' she called as she went in. 'A couple of things I want to talk to Dr Macrae about—' She stopped.

A tall, fair-haired young man, his eyes very blue in the brown of his face, came out of the consulting room.

'Well, now,' he said, 'Uncle Jim didn't tell me about you!'

He held out his hand.

'I'm Neil Patterson. I'm here to give my uncle a hand—and I think I'm going to enjoy doing that!'

There was frank admiration in his blue eyes, an admiration that Meg couldn't help comparing with Adam's cool distance when he'd said that their kiss would be best forgotten.

'Hello, Neil Patterson,' she said. 'I'm Meg Bennett.'

CHAPTER FIVE

DR MACRAE, a mug of coffee in his hand, followed his nephew into the waiting-room.

'Ah—you've met Meg, I see, Neil,' he said. 'Meg, Neil is my youngest sister's laddie—he's just back from North Africa with Médecins Sans Frontières, and his mother thought a wee change would do him good.'

'Rather more than a wee change, I would think, coming to Glen Mor,' Meg said, taking the coffee the young doctor handed to her.

'Well, yes, it's a pretty big change,' Neil agreed. 'My mother is always trying to persuade me to stay in Scotland—she keeps sending me to Uncle Jim when I come home, hoping the glen will tempt me.'

'Aye, well, you're looking a bit more enthusiastic now about being here than you were earlier, laddie,' the old doctor said, straight-faced but with a twinkle in his eyes. 'Now, don't you be holding Meg up. She has a few more folks to see before she picks Jeannie up from school.'

Neil Patterson waited while Meg checked the new list Beth had left for her, and then walked out to the car with her.

'I suppose that was my uncle's tactful way of saying hands off,' he said.

It took Meg a moment to realise what he meant.

'Jeannie isn't my daughter,' she told him. 'I—look after her, that's all.'

She got into the car, and started the engine.

'See you around, then,' the young doctor said, and she waved in answer as she drove off. A pleasant young man,

72

she thought, and she had to smile for that was just the sort of thing her grandmother would say. Yet Neil Patterson did seem very young. But she didn't want to take that thought any further.

Later in the afternoon she drew up at the school gate just as Jeannie came running across the playground, with Colin Cameron beside her.

'So, what about homework?' Meg asked, when the children had finished the milk and home-made biscuits Betsy had ready for them.

There was a quick exchange of glances.

'Yes, we'd better do that right away,' Jeannie said, 'hadn't we, Colin?'

'Oh, yes, that's right, Jeannie,' Colin agreed.

'I think we'll do our homework in my room, Meg,' Jeannie said. 'And when we've finished we're going to be busy, making up a play. Aren't we, Colin?'

Colin's red head nodded.

'That's right,' he confirmed.

'So please don't interrupt us,' Jeannie said, in a businesslike tone. 'We have a lot of practising to do before we show you the play.'

Meg managed to keep her face serious as she agreed that she wouldn't interrupt them.

'Although how much is homework and how much is this play, I don't know,' she said to Adam later when he came back from taking Colin home.

Adam smiled.

'I don't mind,' he said. 'Jeannie is brighter and happier than she has been for—some time. If her homework misses out it doesn't matter. And Colin's mother is pleased—she says he just gets up to mischief at home.'

Every day that week Colin came back to the farm with them, and the children retreated to Jeannie's room. Meg was glad she'd started knitting a pullover for herself, and she sat in the warm kitchen while the children worked on their play.

The old housekeeper was less happy about Colin coming.

'He's a wild wee laddie,' she said suddenly to Meg. 'My brother Archie—that's Colin's grandfather—says he gets away with too much.'

Meg liked the boy, and in spite of her resolve to keep things smooth between Betsy and her she had to defend him.

'Is he not just high-spirited?' she said cautiously.

Betsy sniffed. Meg was able to recognise Betsy's sniffs now, and she thought that this one meant Betsy was prepared to be convinced.

'I don't know what their play is about,' she said, 'but they're certainly working very hard on it. There's hardly a sound from them.'

The old housekeeper shook her head.

'Well, maybe our Jeannie will be a good influence on him,' she said grudgingly.

Meg looked at her, and wondered if she dared say something that was on her mind.

'Betsy,' she said carefully, 'you seem to be short of breath sometimes. Are you feeling all right?'

Betsy's normally high colour became even higher.

'I'm fine,' she said brusquely. 'There's nothing wrong with me, nothing at all. I've always been able to look after things for Adam, and I'm still well able to do that.'

It was wiser to leave it at that, Meg thought, but she was still concerned about the old housekeeper.

The next afternoon, running short of wool, she went up to her room to get more. They're very quiet, she thought as she went past Jeannie's closed door. Very quiet. Too quiet.

She knocked on the door.

'Jeannie,' she said. 'Sorry to interrupt you, but that programme you liked last week is just coming on, and I wondered if you and Colin would like to come and see it.'

There was no reply.

Meg took a deep breath and opened the door. The room was empty. And the window was just a little open. She opened it further, and looked out. The roof of the porch was just below the window. They must have gone out that way and climbed down, then climbed up again by way of the wall into Jeannie's room and then come down to the kitchen. But where had they gone?

There was no need to wonder. She knew very well where they had gone. She hurried downstairs, and took her anorak off the peg.

'I'm going out for a walk, Betsy,' she said. 'Jeannie and Colin are—are still busy.'

She walked across the farmyard and onto the path that led to the low foothills and the caves where Jeannie was so certain she had seen Glen. Meg was breathless by the time she turned off the path, the way Jeannie had come the other day.

As she was about to turn further into the hills she heard voices. Slowly, hoping her feet were silent on the rough grass, she went closer.

They were kneeling on the grass, Jeannie and Colin. A few yards from them, a black and white collie was lying down, his nose on his paws, his eyes on the children.

'Come on, then, Glen, that's a good boy,' Jeannie said softly. 'We'll not hurt you, you know that. It's your own Jeannie, Glen, come back to you.'

Suddenly the dog stiffened and stood up, his head turned towards Meg. In one swift movement he turned and ran away. The children whirled round as Meg came towards them.

'You frightened him away, and he was just going to come to us,' Jeannie accused her, close to tears.

'You've been coming here every day, haven't you?' Meg said.

Jeannie turned away, but Colin lifted his red head high.

'Aye, we have,' he said defiantly. 'We've been bringing food to Glen. He wouldna' take it at first so we just left it. But if you hadna' come now Jeannie would have got him to come right to us.'

Jeannie's small shoulders were shaking, and when Meg took her in her arms and turned the child round silent tears were running down her cheeks.

'Thon dog's no' a killer,' Colin said passionately. 'They're wrong, all of them.'

'Oh, Jeannie, what are we to do?' Meg murmured, holding the little girl close to her. 'You know what your father said.'

Jeannie nodded.

'Please don't tell him, Meg,' she pleaded. 'He—he might feel he has to tell Mr Ferguson where Glen is, and then— and then—Please don't tell him!'

With many misgivings, Meg agreed not to tell Adam.

'At least not yet,' she qualified. 'I have to think about the best thing to do. Meanwhile, you are not to come here again, not—not until I have time to think about what we should do.'

It wasn't right, she knew, to keep this from Adam, and yet Jeannie was right. If he knew he might well feel that he had to tell Gavin Ferguson.

Jeannie and Colin were both subdued as they went back to the farm, but Meg could see that they had accepted her ruling. She managed to get them inside and up to Jeannie's room, without Betsy seeing or hearing, and that, too, made her feel bad. If Adam knew the extent of her deception he would be very angry. Rightly, she reminded herself.

'Pity you went oot,' the old housekeeper said when she came through from her room, and found Meg sitting innocently knitting. 'Helen Ferguson was here, and looking so bonny.'

Meg didn't look up from her knitting.

'I thought she would have stayed until Adam came in,' she said. Then, taking a chance, she added, 'And didn't she want to see Jeannie? You were saying how fond Helen is of her.'

'She was maybe in a bit of a hurry,' Betsy said quickly. Thank goodness she didn't want to see Jeannie, Meg found herself thinking. 'Anyway, she left a message to let Adam know she's going back to Inverness, but she'll be here next weekend.'

A message that she could easily have left by telephone, Meg thought. I bet she just wanted to establish her claim on Adam!

Taken aback by the ferocity of that unbidden thought, she reminded herself that it was nothing to her whether or not Helen Ferguson felt she had any claim on Adam Kerr.

The next morning, when she reached the surgery, after doing some home visits for the district nurse, she found Neil Patterson in charge.

'I sent my uncle off, fishing,' he told her cheerfully. 'He can do with a bit of relaxing, and he never manages to find the time. Aunt Sheena packed him a picnic, and we told him to take the whole day. Beth is out so, if you don't mind, I can use some help with the patients. Who do we have first?'

Meg had already glanced at the full waiting-room and begun to get the cards ready.

'Andrew Ritchie,' she said. 'Chronic ulcer.'

She gave the young doctor the card, and went to bring Andrew Ritchie in.

'Oh, it's yourself, young Neil, is it?' the white-haired man said. 'Fancy you being a real doctor now, and me remembering you coming and playing in the burn as a wee laddie. Just a few more of the white pills Dr Macrae gives me and I'll be fine. They keep this ulcer from doing any more complaining.'

Neil looked at the card, and then looked at the man in front of him. 'I was up at the hotel last night, Andrew,' he said easily. 'Did I not catch a glimpse of you through in the bar?'

The old man looked down at his gnarled hands, which were interlaced.

'Well, now, you might have done,' he said thoughtfully. 'I just went in to see Rory Campbell about something.'

The young doctor shook his head. 'And what use is it, giving you more white pills, Andrew, to keep your ulcer quiet, and then you irritate it with a drink?'

The blue eyes gazing into his were guileless.

'Aye, well,' the old man murmured, 'you could be right, and you with all the book learning you must have. I will be thinking about what you have just said, young Neil.'

When he had gone Neil shook his head. 'Uncle Jim has been treating Andrew's ulcer for years, and Andrew has been mistreating it,' he said. 'Some day we'll have real trouble with it. Right—who do we have next?'

Together they worked through the waiting patients. Under Neil Patterson's direction, Meg took out stitches, bandaged, took temperatures and checked a patient's insulin level. She couldn't help admitting that, in spite of the young doctor's carefree approach, he was thoroughly professional. And experienced.

'I can see you've had a lot of experience in dealing with busy waiting-rooms quickly and efficiently, Neil,' she said, when they were having a quick cup of coffee.

'It's certainly different here from being in the Sudan, but, yes, out there we have so many people coming from miles around that we have to work quickly.'

He took a bite out of his aunt's shortbread biscuits appreciatively.

'I've sometimes thought I'd like to go somewhere like that for a couple of years,' Meg said.

'You're just the kind of person we need out there, Meg,' Neil said eagerly. 'When I go to London for my next briefing I could get you some forms to fill in.'

Meg shook her head.

'Not right now, I'm afraid. I'm—committed to being here with Jeannie for now.'

He nodded.

'Uncle Jim told me about her,' he said quietly. 'I know her father doesn't want people to know, but while I'm here I might have to see her. How is she at the moment?'

Meg told him that she was fine, and in remission. 'But...' She hesitated.

'Yes, there's always a "but" in a case like that, isn't there?' the young doctor said, and the sympathy in his voice, along with what she had seen of the way he worked, impressed Meg. Yes, she thought, he is young, but maybe not as young as I thought.

He came out with her when she left, and they stood, talking, beside the car for a little while before Meg went off to collect Jeannie from school.

Jeannie, and Colin with her.

'And we really are going to do a play,' Jeannie said. 'A play about Bonny Prince Charlie. Do you know, Meg, he hid in a cave here in the glen when he was escaping?'

'So they say,' Colin said scornfully. 'But my dad says if Bonny Prince Charlie had hidden in every cave he's suppose to have hidden in, he would be here to this day. Anyway,' he added hastily, 'I don't mind doing a play about him, even if I don't believe in him hiding here in the glen.'

That night, when Adam came back from taking Colin

home, he said he was looking forward to seeing the play. Meg was all too conscious of the slight flush on Jeannie's cheeks, as she said that they still had to do some work on it.

'Speaking of work,' Adam said easily, turning to Meg, 'I see Dr Macrae's nephew is back here again. You'll be finding him interesting to work with, I suppose, and him with all that experience in the Sudan. The two of you certainly seemed to be having a good talk when I passed down the road this afternoon.'

Now Meg could feel her own cheeks warm with colour. 'I didn't see you passing,' she said.

Adam's dark eyes rested on her for a long time.

'No,' he said thoughtfully. 'No, I didn't think you would be seeing me.' He smiled, but it was a smile that didn't reach his eyes. 'You would enjoy meeting someone who comes from your own world, Meg,' he said.

Meg wasn't sure whether he meant the world of medicine or the wider world outside the glen, but somehow she couldn't keep herself from thinking of what he'd said, and of the way he'd said it.

It had been a comment, nothing more, she told herself. It was foolish to think that Adam had been disturbed in any way because of seeing her with Neil Patterson. And it was even more foolish for her to let such a thought come into her mind.

It was a wet weekend, and Adam was busy in his office for most of the time. Jeannie was quiet, a little withdrawn, but that didn't surprise Meg for she knew very well that the little girl would be thinking of her dog, hiding in the cave in the hills.

She herself was thinking of the deserted beach a week ago—Jeannie, with the dog beside her, away in the distance, and Adam's lips hard on hers, his arms holding her

so close to him. Dangerously close, she knew that very
well.

She kept remembering, too, his deep, dark voice, and the
story of the silkies. What was it he'd said when the story
was over? 'But surely a man should have more sense than
to keep a seal-woman away from the sea, to keep her in a
place that is not meant for her?'

'Meg.'

Jeannie's voice broke into her disturbing thoughts. She
turned to the child, standing at the door of her room.

'Meg,' Jeannie said quickly, 'I know I promised I
wouldn't go, but—but we've been taking food for Glen all
week, and he must be hungry. I wondered...'

Meg waited.

'I wondered,' Jeannie said, in a small voice, 'if you
would take this bag of biscuits and just put it inside the
cave. I found it in the larder. There was another one, but
it's finished. Colin will take food, but he can't get away at
the weekend.'

I shouldn't have agreed, Meg thought a little later as she
trudged up the hill, her anorak buttoned tightly, the rain
driving into her face. What on earth would Adam say if he
knew?

There was no sign of the dog when she reached the cave,
although she thought she saw a movement in the darkness
at the back. She emptied the big bag of biscuits, well out
of sight of the opening to the cave, and then, softly, she
called the dog's name.

'No, he wouldn't come. He doesn't know you,' Jeannie
said, when Meg got back. 'But he'll find it. Thank you,
Meg—thank you so much.'

Her arms were warm around Meg's neck, and her cheek
soft against Meg's. Meg returned the hug, glad to see that
Jeannie looked brighter, knowing that the dog had food.

*   *   *

On Monday morning, when Meg woke and went through as usual to tell Jeannie it was time to get up, she could see immediately that Jeannie wasn't well. There were dark shadows under her grey eyes, and she was even paler than usual.

Meg's heart turned over as Jeannie looked up at her, not saying anything. She sat on the bed.

'I don't feel very well, Meg,' Jeannie said.

'I can see that,' Meg replied. She put her hand on Jeannie's forehead, not even needing to do any more to know that she had a temperature. She said carefully, 'What doesn't feel right, Jeannie?'

'My head's sore, and my legs feel tired. And my tummy's a bit sore, like it was when I was ill before.'

Meg kissed the soft cheek, and tucked the duvet closer around Jeannie.

'I think you'd better stay right where you are,' she said, and she hoped her voice sounded bright and cheerful. She looked out the window. 'Still raining—not a bad day to stay off school, Jeannie.'

Jeannie sat up.

'I have to go to school,' she said urgently. 'I have to see Colin to tell him that you took food to Glen yesterday.'

Gently but firmly Meg made Jeannie lie down.

'I'll let Colin know,' she said, although she didn't know how she would do that. She thought of something, and she could see that Jeannie had thought of it too.

'Colin didn't promise he wouldn't go,' she said quickly. 'He crossed his fingers so that the promise doesn't count.'

Meg stood. 'I'll bring you something to eat,' she said.

'I'm not really hungry,' Jeannie said.

'I know, but just some tea and toast,' Meg told her.

She went downstairs, still in her dressing-gown. Adam was always out early, coming back for breakfast, and he had just come in. He was sitting at the fire, a mug of tea in his hand and the dog at his feet.

'Adam,' Meg said.

He looked up, obviously surprised to see her in her dressing-gown.

'I didn't hear you,' he said.

There was no easy way to say this, Meg knew.

'Jeannie isn't well, Adam,' she said quietly.

'She was all right yesterday. Maybe she's just tired, or…' He stopped, his eyes searching her face for the truth he didn't want to face. A truth he would have to face, Meg knew, her heart heavy.

'I think she should see Dr Macrae,' she said.

CHAPTER SIX

ADAM had reached the door before Meg caught up with him and put her hand on his arm.

'Don't alarm her, Adam,' she said, and the urgency of her voice must have got through to him. 'I just said to her she'd better stay off school today.'

He looked down at her, his dark eyes bleak.

'You're right, of course,' he said, his voice low. 'I shouldn't go up to her like this, should I?'

'No, you shouldn't,' Meg agreed steadily. 'Just take a few deep breaths, and calm down.'

With an effort that hurt her to see, he managed to smile.

'Jeannie was right,' he said, 'you are bossy. I'm fine now, Meg. I'll go up and see her.'

Meg stood at the foot of the stairs, listening, as Adam went into Jeannie's room and spoke to her. When he came down he stopped, seeing her waiting.

'How did I do?' he asked.

'You were just right,' she assured him. 'Not too casual, but not too worried either.'

They went back into the kitchen and, without asking her, he poured a cup of tea for her from the big teapot at the side of the stove.

'What now?' he asked her. 'Is there anything that can be done?'

'Yes, there is,' Meg replied with a confidence that she hoped and prayed would be justified. 'She'll probably need one or more transfusions of platelets and red cells. But the first thing is a blood test—would you like me to phone Dr Macrae?'

It was Neil Patterson who answered, and he told her that the old doctor was out, delivering a baby.

'It's Jeannie,' Meg told him. She described the child's symptoms, and said that they could wait until Dr Macrae could come.

'I think I should come, Meg,' Neil said. 'The sooner we send off blood for testing the better. I'll be along right away.'

Betsy made toast for Jeannie, and Meg took a tray up to her. Adam was sitting in the chair beside the bed, and he rose and took the tray from Meg.

'You'd better eat it, Jeannie,' Meg said, as Jeannie's small nose wrinkled at the sight of the toast. 'I'm not very brave where Betsy is concerned, and I daren't face her if there's toast left on the plate.' Then, casually, she said that Dr Patterson was coming as Dr Macrae was busy, delivering a baby.

'I'll wait and see him, too,' Adam said, after a moment's pause, which told Meg fairly clearly that he would rather it had been the old doctor coming.

'You can go back to the fire, Daddy,' Jeannie said. 'Meg will stay with me, won't you, Meg?' She added hastily, 'It isn't that I need someone to be with me, it's just for company.'

When her father had gone she turned to Meg.

'You will tell Colin not to go to see Glen, Meg?' she whispered urgently. 'We did go every day, but we were thinking we shouldn't in case someone sees us and follows us. So tell Colin not to go for a few days, and then I'll be better and...and...' Her voice faltered.

Meg wasn't to be drawn into any discussion of whether or not Jeannie would be going to the cave. As it had turned out, she thought with sadness, that was something that wouldn't happen now that Jeannie was ill.

'And, Meg, we took Rex's food from the pantry, and Betsy or Daddy will look for it. You can get it in the shop.'

Meg wrote down what she had to get, and she could see that Jeannie was less agitated now that she had agreed to do this. She took the tray, with most of the toast finished, but at the door she turned.

'What has Glen been living on, I wonder, for all these months?' she asked.

'Colin thinks he's been stealing from people's rubbish,' Jeannie said. 'His mum sometimes finds their bin turned over, and so do other people.'

'It was certainly possible, Meg thought as she went downstairs. She heard a car draw up, and all thoughts of the dog left her as she hurried to let Neil Patterson in.

Adam rose when she took the young doctor into the kitchen.

'Hello, Adam,' Neil said. 'Quite a while since I've seen you. You and Jeannie were away last time I was in the glen.'

'Yes, we were in Switzerland and in America,' Adam replied. 'You know about Jeannie's illness?'

Neil Patterson nodded.

'Uncle Jim thought I should be in the picture, in case I had to see her,' he said. 'And I think he felt I might have come across some new research he hadn't heard about. Let me have a look at Jeannie, and we'll take it from there.'

'I'll stay here,' Adam said. 'You go up, Meg.'

The young doctor's swift and professional examination of Jeannie confirmed all that Meg had been finding about him as she'd worked with him.

'Sorry about this, Jeannie, but we need to take a blood test,' Neil said.

'I don't like blood tests,' Jeannie said, more than a little mutinously. 'I had an awful lot of them when I was in hospital in Inverness and when we were away.'

'I've yet to meet anyone who jumps up and down for joy when I say we need a blood test,' Neil told her. 'That's right—Meg, keep her arm steady. Real Scottish blood, Jeannie, reluctant to come. Now, how bad was that, Jeannie?'

'Not so bad as some I've had,' Jeannie admitted. She smiled, a rather wobbly little smile but still, Meg thought, relieved, a smile. 'But I'm not jumping for joy, Dr Patterson.'

Neil put the syringe in its sterile bag, and closed his case.

'I think you'd better have a few days off school, Jeannie,' he said, 'until we find out what's going on. And I suppose this means you're taking Meg away from us at the surgery? Oh, well, we'll have to manage.'

Adam Kerr rose when they went into the kitchen.

'Well?' he said brusquely. 'How is she?'

Neil put down his bag. 'It certainly looks as if the remission is over,' he said carefully. 'Her spleen and her liver are slightly enlarged, but the blood count will tell us what we need to know. It will probably mean the hospital in Inverness and a transfusion of platelets and red cells. Thanks, Meg.' He took the cup of tea Meg had poured for him, and sat down.

'She'll be given antibiotics, as well as some of the specific leukaemia drugs. As many of these drugs are toxic to normal marrow cells we're going to have to be very careful about infection of any kind. But you'll have heard all this before, Adam.'

Adam's dark eyes were bleak, his jaw a hard line, as he nodded.

'I should have known it was too good to last,' he said, his voice low.

'Adam,' the young doctor said firmly, 'don't you be giving up. It's the worst thing for you and for Jeannie. With the sort of treatment I've just spoken about, she may well go into remission again. And there is research being done all the time. Someone, somewhere, may come up with the right drug to help Jeannie.'

He stood, and turned to Meg.

'Keep her in bed until we get the results of the blood test. We don't want to do any damage to that spleen in its enlarged state. I'm not prescribing anything at the moment. If her temperature rises, back to the old-fashioned sponging to bring it down. And try to keep your concern to yourselves. Keep Jeannie as calm as possible. I'll let you know as soon as we have the results.'

Meg went out to his car with him. As he opened the door he smiled down at her.

'I did get a bit technical, I'm afraid,' he said, 'but I think Adam still sees me as the wee laddie who used to come to the glen for his holidays so I had to reassure him.'

'You did pretty well,' Meg told him. She waved to him as he drove off, and then went back into the house to find Adam telling Betsy that the doctor thought Jeannie should stay in bed for a few days.

When Betsy went out of the kitchen, Meg said, 'Adam, don't you think Betsy should know? She's known Jeannie all her life, and she'll worry more, not knowing. I'm sure she wouldn't say a word to anyone else.'

Adam didn't say anything. All at once, with an intuitive understanding that shook her later when she thought about it, Meg went over to him and put a hand on his arm.

'Adam,' she said gently, 'telling Betsy won't make it any more or less real, you know.'

He looked down at her, his eyes very dark, and then he sighed.

'Yes, it is foolish,' he said, his voice low, 'to be thinking that the less I speak about it the less real it will be. But we'll wait until the result of the blood test comes, I think, until we know what is to be done, before Betsy needs to know. I'm sorry you will not be able to be helping at the surgery, Meg, for I know how much you have been enjoying that.'

Meg shook her head.

'That doesn't matter, Adam,' she said, meaning it. 'I came here to look after Jeannie, and now I'm needed to do that. There is one thing, though.'

She'd been wondering how she was going to manage to get to the village to do what Jeannie wanted her to do, and now she'd thought of a way to do it. She reminded Adam that the doctor had said they were to keep Jeannie calm, and she said that Jeannie was worried about her homework.

'I'm sure she'll have a sleep later in the morning, and I could go to the school and talk to her teacher. I think it would reassure Jeannie,' she said.

Adam agreed that it would be a good idea and Meg felt a wave of shame at the way she was deceiving him. Let us get sorted out with Jeannie, she promised herself, and I'll deal with the rest of it. Even if it means owning up to Adam.

She told Jeannie what she was going to do and, as she had hoped, Jeannie fell asleep in the middle of the morning.

'I've given her the little handbell, Betsy,' Meg said, when she went downstairs. 'She'll ring if she needs anything, but I don't think you'll be bothered.'

It had been the wrong choice of words, she realised as the old housekeeper bristled.

'And why would it be a bother to me,' she said indignantly, 'and me looked after Jeannie all her life? I may not be young, but I can still look after a bairn that needs me!'

Precious time had to be spent reassuring Betsy that, of course, Meg knew that Jeannie was no bother to her.

It was strange, she thought, being in the village and not in uniform.

'Hello, Nurse, not working today?' Mrs Farquhar in the shop asked when Meg bought the dry dog food.

'No,' Meg told her. 'Jeannie isn't very well so she's not at school. I'm just off there to see about her homework.'

'Homework, now?' The grey head shook in amazement. 'I wish my wee grandson would bother a bit more about homework.'

Well, Meg consoled herself, Jeannie is a conscientious child. She'd want to do homework if she felt well enough.

Jeannie's teacher agreed as she wrote out some homework for Jeannie, and nodded as Meg said guardedly that, of course, doing it would depend on how Jeannie felt.

'Yes, you can have a word with Colin,' she said, a little surprised. 'Colin, Nurse Bennett wants to talk to you—you can go outside with her.'

In the corridor Meg told Colin what Jeannie had said. The red head nodded.

'I thought she was off because her daddy had found out about Glen,' Colin said. 'Tell her I hope she'll be better soon. And she's not to worry. Come Thursday, I'll take some food to him and I'll be awful careful no' to be seen.'

He smiled engagingly, his small freckled nose wrinkling.

'You were awful brave, Meg, to go and take food to Glen. What if Jeannie's daddy had seen you?'

Meg took Colin's messages back to Jeannie, and the little girl looked brighter. It's the only thing I can do for her, Meg told herself. Put her mind at rest as much as possible.

The few days of waiting for the results of the blood test seemed very long to Meg. Jeannie was alarmingly tired, and her small face looked more drained each day. Meg had half expected the little girl to object to having to stay in bed, but Jeannie didn't ask if she could get up. Adam carried an old rocking-chair from the kitchen up to her room, and Meg sat there most of the time, talking when Jeannie wanted her to talk but otherwise just sitting there.

'Tell me about when you were a little girl, Meg,' Jeannie asked more than once, and Meg brought out memories of her childhood to offer to Jeannie.

'So you were like me—an only child,' she said in an old-fashioned way, which brought an unexpected blur of tears to Meg's eyes.

'Yes, but I was lucky. I had cousins living near, and we were together a lot,' Meg told her. 'My cousin Laura and I were like sisters—we still are, although she's a few years older than I am. She has two little girls about your age, Jeannie.'

'And they're the ones you read *The Last Dragon* to,' Jeannie said, her voice blurred with weariness. 'Can we read it again, Meg?'

Meg sat quietly beside her as Jeannie fell asleep halfway through the story.

'Meg,' Adam said softly from the door. 'Betsy has a cottage pie ready—come down and have something to eat.'

'I'll bring a tray up and have it here,' Meg said. 'I think she likes to know I'm here when she wakes.'

Adam took the book from her hands, and drew her to her feet.

'For once I'm the one to be bossy,' he said firmly. 'You are to come down and have your food in the kitchen. I've poured a glass of wine for you.'

A little later, sitting in the warmth of the kitchen, with the dog asleep beside the big stove, he said to her, 'Do you always become this attached to your patients, Meg? I thought nurses had to keep at a distance.'

Meg thought about that.

'I've never been in a one-to-one position like this before,' she said at last. 'That makes a difference. But, yes, Adam, Jeannie has become very special to me.'

His eyes were very dark.

'And you have become very special to her,' he said, his voice low. 'She has never had any relationship like this—she was too young when her mother died.'

He had talked only briefly about his wife, and Meg had never felt she'd had the right to ask any more. Now, in the warmth of the kitchen, with their shared concern for the child asleep in her room, it seemed a natural thing to do.

'It must have been very hard for you, being left on your own with such a young child,' she said quietly.

'It wasn't easy,' the big man admitted. 'It seemed that we'd had such a short time together, Shelagh and I—and Jeannie. It's a lonely life, farming in a glen like this, Meg. When we were first married Shelagh was so bright, always laughing. For a long time, after she died it was as if someone had switched off a light in my life. For Jeannie as well as for me. But, well, it's a long time ago now, and I've got used to being on my own. Although...'

He paused, and for some reason Meg's heart turned over. Before he could say any more the phone rang. Adam left the door to the hall open when he hurried through, and Meg had no option but to hear what he said.

'Helen? Oh—yes, you did ask me to ring you. I'm afraid I forgot.' There was a pause, and then he said carefully, 'No, it was because Jeannie is ill. I'd rather not make any arrangements, Helen, until I see how she is.' Another pause. 'Well, you just go with the others. Fine you know these dinner dances in posh hotels are not really my scene!'

He came back through and said, a little brusquely, that he would go up and see if Jeannie was awake.

It was Thursday before the results of Jeannie's blood test came back. Neil phoned to say he would look in at lunchtime if Adam would be there then.

The young doctor wasted no time, and Meg could see that Adam was as grateful as she was for that.

'The peripheral blood shows anaemia and an elevated white cell count,' he said quietly. 'There may be organ infiltration—the enlarged spleen indicates that. She has to go to hospital, Adam. They'll give her a transfusion of platelets and red blood cells.' He paused, and added that that should make a big difference to Jeannie's condition.

'But there's no guarantee,' Adam said flatly.

'No, there's no guarantee, but there's a pretty good chance, Adam.' He stood. 'I think I should tell Jeannie myself. Can you take her through tomorrow, Adam? There's a bed ready for her in the children's ward.'

Adam and Meg went up with him to Jeannie's room. The little girl listened quietly as the doctor told her that she would have to go to hospital in Inverness, where they would help her to feel a lot better.

'When am I going?' she asked, and it was her father who told her she would be going the next day.

She looked at him. 'But, Daddy, it's lambing time—you can't be away from the farm.'

'I can manage the day away, lass, to take you there,' Adam told her. He looked at Meg. 'I was wondering, Meg, if you would stay in Inverness while Jeannie is in hospital? There's a cousin of Beth Drummond's who lives near, and she takes in B and Bs—you could stay there.'

'Of course I'll do that,' Meg said.

'Don't worry, Jeannie,' Neil said, turning as he reached the door. 'They're nice folks in the hospital there.'

But Meg knew very well that Jeannie's look of anguish wasn't for the stay in hospital. 'I'll get a message to Colin somehow, Jeannie,' she whispered, when Adam and the young doctor had gone downstairs, although she had no idea how she would manage that.

Later that afternoon she heard Betsy's raised voice, and

Colin's as well. She hurried downstairs, to find Betsy closing the door on the small red-headed boy.

'I said she's no' weel,' she said firmly. 'She's away to the hospital tomorrow, and she'll not be wanting to see you, Colin Cameron.'

'But, Auntie Betsy…'

His great-aunt shook her head. 'You heard what I said.'

Meg took a deep breath, and intervened. 'I don't think a little visit from Colin will do Jeannie any harm at all, Betsy,' she said. 'Just for a few minutes, Colin. He's come all this way. That was nice of you, Colin.'

'Och, well, you're the nurse,' Betsy grumbled, and turned away.

The little boy's usual exuberance deserted him when he saw Jeannie in bed. He turned to Meg with distress in his eyes.

'Jeannie was worried about having to go to hospital, Colin,' Meg said quickly. 'Because of Glen.'

'I've just been to the cave, Jeannie,' Colin said. 'No, I didn't see him, but he's eaten all the food that was there and I've left more. I'll take some more maybe at the weekend, and I'll be very careful.'

Meg gave him money to buy more food, not caring that she was compounding her earlier wrongs. Anything, she thought, to give Jeannie peace of mind.

'Thank you, Colin,' Jeannie said. 'Mind and be careful, now.'

Meg took the little boy back downstairs.

'I'm sure your Auntie Betsy won't see you going all that way back without a drink of milk and a biscuit,' she said, but the old housekeeper had already set out that very thing on the kitchen table.

'I see you're on your bike, laddie,' she said, when he'd finished. 'Be careful, now, on the way home.'

In spite of what she says, she's very fond of him, Meg thought as the old lady handed the boy his anorak.

Outside, as Colin was ready to go, he looked up at her. 'Jeannie really isn't well, Meg,' he said, not quite steadily, 'but she'll be better when she comes home from the hospital, won't she?'

It took a moment or two before Meg answered him, as his eyes searched her face.

'Yes, Colin,' she said at last. 'Yes, I'm sure she will be.'

But as the little boy cycled off Meg thought, with a weight of sadness in her heart, I hope and pray that it's true.

CHAPTER SEVEN

MEG remembered very little of the journey to Inverness the next day.

They made a bed for Jeannie on the back seat, and she slept for most of the way. Adam and Meg didn't talk much—partly so as not to disturb the sleeping child and partly because their hearts were too heavy for talking.

Just before they reached Inverness Jeannie woke up.

'Daddy,' she said, 'when they've done this blood thing that Dr Patterson said, I can come home right away, can't I?'

Adam's eyes left the road just long enough to meet Meg's. They had talked until late last night, and eventually he had agreed that, without giving a child of ten the whole bleak picture, he should be as honest as possible with her.

'We're not sure about that, lass,' he said, 'not until the doctors at the hospital here have a talk about the best thing to do.'

Jeannie sighed.

'I thought I was better,' she said, 'but this is like when I was ill before.' She sat up and leaned forward, her fair head, sleep-rumpled, coming between them. 'Daddy, even if I don't feel better please don't let's go back to these other hospitals. I just want to go home to the farm, and I don't ever want to go away again.'

Meg could see that the urgency of her voice startled her father. This isn't fair to Adam, she thought with certainty. I have to tell him about the dog, but this wasn't the time.

'I thought you wanted to go back to Disneyworld, Jeannie,' she said, as lightly as she could.

'Well, maybe just there,' Jeannie agreed, ''cos I'd like you to be with us next time, Meg, specially for the dolls. You didn't really appreciate the dolls, did you, Daddy?'

Adam agreed that he hadn't.

'Look,' he said. 'Inverness. Is it not a bonny city, with the River Ness cutting through the old town with the red sandstone buildings? And there is Castlehill—the view from there will take the breath from your body. You'll never have been here, Meg?'

'I'd never been in Scotland at all until I came with you and Jeannie,' Meg told him.

'Och, well, I must admit I haven't seen much of England—nor felt the need to,' Adam said, straight-faced, and Jeannie gave a little giggle. Meg, all too conscious of the effort Adam was making to lighten things, assured Jeannie that her feelings weren't really hurt—she was only pretending.

The hospital had the look and the smell and the feel of every hospital Meg had known and worked in, and she found that reassuring. The children's oncology ward was bright and cheerful, the nurses brisk and professional but with the warmth Meg knew was so necessary in nursing children.

'Dr Robinson is going to do some tests, Jeannie,' the sister in charge said. 'Now, how about we send Daddy away for a little while, and Mummy can stay with you?'

Adam's eyes, startled, met Meg's, and Meg felt her cheeks grow warm. It had been a natural misunderstanding.

'She isn't my mummy, she's Meg,' Jeannie said, matter-of-factly. 'And she's a nurse too.'

'Well, then, she'll know just what Dr Robinson is doing, won't she?' the sister said briskly. But her eyes moved speculatively from Meg to Adam. Rather to Meg's surprise, Adam didn't seem to be in any hurry to set the record straight so she said hastily that she was looking after Jeannie.

It was strange, though, she thought during the next hour as Jeannie's tests were done, that, in fact, she wasn't really able to keep a professional distance. This wasn't just any patient, any child—this was Jeannie.

She had seen a number of bone-marrow aspirations done, and she knew the procedure—the cleansed skin area anaesthetised, the bone-marrow needle introduced. When it entered the marrow cavity a syringe was attached and a small volume of blood and marrow aspirated. She knew from her training that there would be brief pain at the actual aspiration, and Jeannie had been warned about that, but for the first time Meg could almost feel that pain as silent tears came into Jeannie's eyes.

'I'm sorry about that one,' the grey-haired doctor said. 'It's nasty, isn't it?'

'Yes, it is,' Jeannie agreed, drowsy from the sedative she had been given. She tried to smile, and her hand held Meg's even more tightly. 'It was worse last time. I'm glad you're with me, Meg.'

It was early evening before the transfusion of red cells and platelets was begun. The young nurse in charge kept monitoring the rate of infusion, Jeannie's pulse and temperature. She would, Meg knew, be alert to any allergic reaction or to the possibility of circulatory overloading.

Adam had looked in a few times, and when the transfusion was complete he came in and sat beside Meg.

'It's past visiting time, but you can stay until Jeannie goes to sleep,' the sister told them.

'I thought you were going back to the farm, Daddy, for the lambing,' Jeannie murmured drowsily.

'I'll leave early in the morning,' Adam said. 'I'm going to stay at Elspeth Ritchie's tonight. I wanted to stay to see the doctor and hear what he's going to do.'

Jeannie's eyes opened. 'You mean this blood thing isn't all?' she asked.

Adam took her small hand in his. 'I'm afraid not, lass,' he said gently. 'There will be more pills, and they want to make sure the pills are agreeing with you before you come home.'

Chemotherapy was necessary, Dr Robinson had said, and he had to monitor Jeannie's reaction.

'Meg will stay,' Adam told the little girl. 'She's going to stay at Mrs Ritchie's, and she'll be able to walk along here every day to see you. When you're ready to come home I'll come and take you both back.'

Jeannie fell asleep soon after that, and Adam and Meg left. They walked back to the big old house where they were to stay, and Meg was glad of the cool and fresh air after the hours spent in the hospital.

'I was hoping she wouldn't need the chemotherapy,' Adam said, as they walked out of the hospital gates.

'You know what Dr Robinson said,' Meg reminded him. 'Hit this with everything possible, and there's a good chance she'll go into remission again.'

Under the light of a streetlamp he stopped, and looked down at her.

'I'm so glad you're here with her, Meg,' he said quietly. Then he added, even more quietly, 'With us.'

He took her hand in his, and kept it there as they walked along the street.

Elspeth Ritchie was very like her cousin Beth, and she made Meg feel very much at home.

'You'll not have had anything to eat, I'm sure, so I've warmed up a stew for you. Sit here in this little sitting-room, just the two of you. I have one or two other folks staying, but they're all next door, watching TV. I'll just leave you on your own now that you know where your rooms are.'

Meg hadn't thought that she was hungry, but to her surprise, she enjoyed the stew, and the potatoes and lightly done vegetables. There was also tea and home-made fruit-cake, and she was glad to see that Adam ate well too.

When they'd finished Meg took the tray through to the kitchen. Perhaps, she thought, this was the time to tell Adam about Jeannie and Colin, feeding the dog. Her own part in it, too, had to be told.

But when she went back into the small sitting-room Adam was asleep.

Gently, Meg closed the door. Adam's dark head was leaning awkwardly on a cushion, his dark lashes on his brown cheeks. They were ridiculously long lashes for a man, Meg thought. His chin was dark, for it had been very early when he'd shaved. Tired and worried as he was, somehow asleep he looked younger, defenceless. Vulnerable.

She moved the cushion carefully to make him more comfortable, but he opened his eyes as she was doing so. For an endless moment, it seemed to her, his eyes held hers, and in the silence of the room she could hear the uneven thudding of her heart. Or was it his?

'I'm sorry, Meg,' Adam said, his voice blurred with weariness. 'I didn't sleep much last night. But you probably didn't either. We'd best get off to bed.'

I'm a coward, Meg told herself, but I'm not going to tell him about the dog now.

Their rooms were next door to each other, and on the landing outside Meg's door Adam looked down at her. Very gently, he touched her cheek with one hand.

'Goodnight, Meg,' he said softly.

'Goodnight, Adam,' she whispered.

Tired as she was, she hadn't expected to fall asleep so

quickly, and to sleep so soundly. She woke to the sound of the Land Rover's engine, below in the quiet street, and she reached the window in time to see the tail-lights, disappearing round the corner. Adam had said he would leave early, but she couldn't help feeling ridiculously disappointed to have missed him.

She turned, and saw a note just under the door. He hadn't wanted to wake her, he said, and he needed to get back to the farm. Would she phone him every night, and tell him how Jeannie was?

Of course, she told herself, there was no reason why he should have wakened her. It was very thoughtful and sensible of him, with such an early start, to have gone off quietly and left a note. It wouldn't have occurred to him that she might not have minded him waking her up, that she might have wanted to see him and say goodbye to him. And why should it? Determinedly she put such foolish thoughts out of her mind.

That time in Inverness, Meg thought then and later, had a strange and distant sense of disorientation about it. She woke in this strange house, greeted Elspeth and her husband and Beth and John Drummond's children, who lived there during the school term. She had breakfast, and walked along to the hospital. She spent the whole day there, going unwillingly to the cafeteria to have something to eat in the middle of the day and, for the rest of the time, sitting with Jeannie.

The nurses were kind, she found. Not only to her, but to the other people who came here day after day and sat with sick children. They dispensed cups of tea, words of encouragement and constant and warm care for the children.

For the first day or so Jeannie was nauseous, but her drug dosage was adjusted and she looked and felt better. Already the effects of the transfusion could be seen. She had a little colour in her cheeks, and no more dark shadows under her eyes.

'When can I go home?' she asked the doctor impatiently, sitting up in bed when she saw him come in. 'I feel so much better, and Meg can see that I take all my pills. Will I still have to take so many, Dr Robinson?'

'We're going to cut out the big yellow ones before you go home,' the doctor told her. 'I just need a day or so more to check that they've done what I want them to.'

Jeannie nodded.

'To make my blood better,' she said.

Before discharging Jeannie, Dr Robinson took Meg into his office and had a talk with her.

'I'm pleased with Jeannie's progress so far,' he said cautiously. 'She'll be on a combination of drugs for maintenance, and I want to see her in a fortnight. As you know, because many of these drugs are toxic to normal marrow cells a period of marrow aplasia is common during treatment. Jeannie will be under great risk for infections, and I've let Dr Macrae know that she mustn't be treated prophylactically with antibiotics. We need a positive culture and then the appropriate drugs.'

He handed her Jeannie's medication.

'I don't need to tell you this, Miss Bennett, but I will. Look after her, but don't wrap her in cotton wool.'

The next day Adam came to take Meg and Jeannie back to the farm. Meg had brought her small suitcase with her so that they could leave from the hospital. It was a very different journey back. Jeannie sat up, pointing out the castle to Meg and insisting that they should drive down the side of Loch Ness in the hopes of seeing the monster.

'Colin's uncle once saw Nessie, you know, Meg,' she said seriously. 'He was a wee laddie, and he was on a Sunday school picnic. He looked across the loch, and there was a ripple. A huge ripple. And then—' She paused dramatically. 'And then he saw two big humps. The next minute she was gone—under the water—and nobody else from the picnic saw her.'

'And I don't think we are to be lucky today,' her father said. 'We turn away from the loch here, unfortunately. Perhaps another time Nessie will be appearing for us.'

'You don't believe in her. I can tell by your voice, Daddy,' Jeannie said, but she was smiling.

She fell asleep before they reached the glen, and Meg saw the anxiety on Adam's face as he glanced in the mirror.

'She does look tired,' he said, 'and here I was thinking it was like a miracle.'

Meg put her hand over his on the steering-wheel. 'There's no miracle, Adam,' she said, steadily. 'There's a very real improvement, and Dr Robinson says a good chance of remission.' But she is still a very sick little girl, she thought, and she knew, by the tightening of the big farmer's jaw, that there was no need to say the words aloud.

'Well, now, I don't hold with hospitals, but you look a lot better, Jeannie,' the old housekeeper said when they reached the farm. 'Just wait till Rex is back. He's been missing you. Jock looked in to get him, and he says there are three lambs in the field beside the loch.'

Once settled in her room, Jeannie asked Betsy, very casually, if she had seen Colin at all.

'He was here the other day,' Betsy said. 'Came on his bike—said he'd thought he would just look in to see me.' She shook her head, not quite succeeding in hiding a small smile. 'I don't know what's got into the laddie's head, coming all this way just to see his old auntie. It will be my crunchy biscuits he'll be after.'

Meg's eyes met Jeannie's, and Jeannie, too, couldn't quite hide a smile.

'Oh, but Colin's very fond of you, Betsy,' she said. 'I'll be pleased to see him next time he comes.'

That evening, when Jeannie was asleep and Betsy had gone to her room, Adam and Meg sat in the big warm kitchen, and Meg told Adam all that the doctor had said.

'He's been in touch with Dr Macrae, of course, so if there's any need he'll know what to do,' Meg said.

Adam nodded.

'Before, when she was ill, I felt so—alone,' he said slowly. 'It seemed to me there was only me to carry all the weight of Jeannie's illness. Now I don't feel alone because of you, Meg.'

He came over to the couch on which she was sitting and sat beside her. Gently, he cupped her chin in one hand and kissed her. It was a slow, warm kiss, and when at last he released her he smiled.

'And this time,' he said softly, 'I will not be saying that I am sorry for I am not at all sorry.'

Neither am I, Meg thought later in her room. In spite of the ongoing concern about Jeannie, it was a good feeling to be back here at the farm, with Jeannie asleep next door and Adam just along the passage.

Thinking of Adam made her admit that it wasn't very wise, perhaps, this crossing the line between personal life and professional. She had vowed, after Simon, that she would take great care to keep that distance very clearly marked—but this was different. In any case, perhaps she was reading too much into that kiss and the smile that had softened Adam's lean, dark face. Perhaps it had been no more than to show his appreciation for her being there for Jeannie. Yes, that was the way she should look at it—a kiss to say, thanks, I'm glad you're here. No more, no less.

It had been very different from the kiss on the beach. Even the memory of that could bring a warm rush of colour to her cheeks. Disturbing, demanding, and in a moment of complete honesty, like this, Meg knew all too well that no other kiss, no other man, in all her life had made her feel the way she had in Adam's arms. Determinedly, she put that memory out of her mind.

'Do I have to stay in bed?' Jeannie asked the next day, and Meg, with the authority of the doctor in Inverness behind her, agreed that Jeannie could get up for short periods. Both Meg and Jeannie hoped that Colin would come to see Jeannie and bring her news of Glen. But the boy didn't appear, and when Jeannie asked Betsy, very casually, about him she said Colin's mother had kept him off school with a cold for a few days. Jeannie's anguished eyes met Meg's, and later Meg assured her that, as soon as she could, she would try to see Colin and find out about Glen.

Both the old doctor and the young doctor looked in to see Jeannie over the next few days.

'They seem to have got the side-effects of the drug combination under control,' Neil said when Meg went out to his car with him. 'And Jeannie says she could easily get up for longer, but you're too bossy to let her.' His eyes were very blue as he smiled down at her. 'I told her I can believe that.'

'I'm not bossy,' Meg protested. 'Just firm.'

Neil shook his head.

'I tell you, Meg Bennett, you have all the makings of the kind of matron who has young interns shaking in their shoes!'

Meg burst out laughing at this picture of herself. In the middle of her laughter she looked up to see Adam, coming out of the barn.

'Adam, your wee lassie is doing fine,' Neil said, catching sight of the big farmer. 'I'll be back in to see her soon. Bye, Meg.'

Adam must be thinking we were very light-hearted, Neil and I, with Jeannie up there, Meg thought, distressed.

'Adam,' she said, 'Neil was just teasing me about Jeannie saying I'm bossy. He didn't— We weren't—'

Unexpectedly, Adam smiled. 'I'm not an ogre, Meg,' he said. 'I know fine that young Neil is a good and a careful doctor, and it does you good to have a wee while with someone you can be light-hearted with.' He nodded. 'I'm off to the sheep now. Tell Jeannie I'll be back in the middle of the day.'

He whistled for Rex, and strode off across the farmyard.

Meg watched him go. There had been nothing but kindness in Adam's words and in his smile, but it distressed her that he might be thinking there was more between Neil and herself than there really was.

Just why it distressed her so much was something she didn't really want to think about right now.

'She's doing fine, our Jeannie,' the old housekeeper said brightly next day. 'Getting back a bit of colour in her cheeks.'

She and Meg were alone in the kitchen, and Betsy had just come down from Jeannie's room.

'Thank goodness she's finished with the hospital business, although they've sorted her out, right enough. She'll be back at school in no time,' she went on, and now Meg could see that the brightness in her voice was belied by the anxiety in her eyes. She and Adam had talked again of the necessity for Betsy to be told the truth. She hoped that Adam wouldn't feel she should have left it to him, but the time seemed right.

'Betsy,' she said gently, 'Jeannie probably will be back at school soon, but...' There was no easy way to do this. The old woman looked at Meg, and all the pretence at brightness was gone.

'Ye'd better tell me,' she said abruptly. 'But what?'

'But it doesn't mean she's better,' Meg said, her voice steady. 'Sit down, Betsy.'

Without asking, she poured a cup of tea for the house-keeper. Then quietly, honestly, she told her how things were with Jeannie.

When she had finished Betsy Cameron sat for a long time, without speaking. Then, taking Meg completely by surprise, she put her work-worn old hand over Meg's on the table.

'I'm sorry, lass, for the way I was when you came,' she said, not quite steadily. 'I resented you, and I thought there was no need for you when I could look after Jeannie. But, of course, there was a need, and maybe Adam should have told me.' She looked down at her hand on Meg's for a long time, and when she lifted her head her eyes were bright with unshed tears. 'They're saying, the doctors, that all they've managed to do is to give Jeannie a bit more time? That maybe she'll be fine for a bit, and then she'll be ill again?'

Meg nodded, her own throat tight.

'But you never know, do you? And they're not always right, these doctors,' Betsy said, quite aggressively. 'There's some things can happen and give them a surprise.'

'That's true,' Meg replied. 'And there are always new drugs, new treatment, being discovered.' She patted Betsy's hand. 'No, we're not giving up, Betsy—not by any means.'

She stood, and so did the housekeeper. Perhaps this is as good a time as any for me to speak to her about herself, Meg thought.

'Betsy, I'm a little worried about you,' she said carefully. 'I notice sometimes you seem to be breathless.'

'Och, maybe I am, but it's nothing to fuss about,' Betsy muttered, carrying their cups over to the sink.

Meg followed her.

'Is there anything else?' she asked. Following an instinct, then she went on, 'Do you ever have headaches when you get up? And are you more tired than you used to be?'

Betsy busied herself at the sink.

'Maybe I am,' she admitted, 'and a wee thing giddy sometimes. But I dinna hold with doctors, Meg.'

'That's a pity,' Meg said calmly, 'because I think Dr Macrae could prescribe something that would help you to feel better.'

Betsy sniffed, but it was a half-hearted sniff compared with her usual sniffs, Meg thought. After a moment she grudgingly agreed that Meg could phone and make an appointment for her to see the doctor.

That evening, she told Adam that she had talked to Betsy about Jeannie.

'I'm glad you did that,' he said. 'I see now that I should have right at the start, but you were right, Meg. I thought that talking about it was admitting how real it was. And, of course, nothing could change that. Thanks for telling Betsy. I'll have a word with her tomorrow—she'll be away in her room for her favourite programmes now. I'll go up and sit with Jeannie for a wee while. Do you think she could come down here for a change, maybe?'

Afterwards, Meg was to wish that she had taken that chance to tell Adam about the children and the dog, and about her own part in it. But she didn't, and that was something she was to regret for just as Adam was going out of the kitchen to go and bring Jeannie down there was a knock at the back door. He opened it, and Meg looked up from the letter she was writing, to hear him say, 'Gavin—and what brings you out on a night like this? Come in, come in.'

But the neighbouring farmer stood at the door, obviously ill at ease.

'I'm not staying, Adam,' he said abruptly. 'I just came

to tell you that two of my sheep have been killed on the hillside where your farm and mine touch. My shepherd came to tell me, and I got down there right away. I saw him, Adam, at the far end of the field. Your dog. I had my gun, and I got a shot at him.'

Meg found herself standing beside Adam, her hand on his arm. The kitchen was silent, and the dog lying beside the fire stood up, sensing that something was wrong.

'He ran away, but he was limping badly. He'll not have got far,' Gavin Ferguson said. 'I had no choice, Adam, and him just killed the sheep. But I came to tell you because I know he meant a lot to your lassie.'

Adam was white to the lips, but he nodded.

'No, you had no choice, Gavin,' he agreed. 'Did your shepherd actually see him at the sheep?'

The other farmer shook his head. 'No, but the sheep were dead, and the dog was at the far end of the field. Adam, I had to shoot him.'

They all heard the sound at the same time. A small gasp. Jeannie stood at the door to the passage, her hand to her mouth, her grey eyes wide.

'You shot Glen,' she said, and it wasn't a question—it was an accusation.

Adam knelt beside his small daughter and put his arms around her.

'Mr Ferguson had to, Jeannie,' he said. 'There were more sheep killed.'

Jeannie shook her head.

'You said no one actually saw him at the sheep,' she said shakily. 'Glen wouldn't kill sheep, he wouldn't. Tell him that, Daddy.'

Adam stood up.

'I think you'd better go, Gavin,' he said.

The other farmer nodded. At the door he turned.

'I'm sorry, lass,' he said to Jeannie. The door closed behind him.

Adam lifted Jeannie up, and sat her in the big chair beside the stove.

'We can't blame Gavin Ferguson, lass,' he said gently. 'And maybe we can't blame Glen. He was ill-treated, he went wild and…he was hungry. He needed food.'

Jeannie shook her head.

'He didn't need food. We took him food—Colin and me, and Meg, too,' she said passionately. 'He didn't kill the sheep, Daddy. I know he didn't.'

Over her head, Adam's dark eyes met Meg's.

'You did what?' he asked, unbelieving. 'You took food to the dog?'

It would have been bad enough for Adam to learn what had happened, Meg knew, but to learn it in this way…

'I think you'd better tell me everything,' he said tightly.

Jeannie lifted her head.

'It wasn't Meg's fault,' she said. 'It was Colin and me. We found him, and we took him food, and—and then Meg followed us, and she told us we mustn't do it, and…'

Her voice faltered.

'I know we should have told you, Adam,' Meg said, as steadily as she could, 'but Jeannie was afraid you would feel you had to tell Gavin Ferguson. And I took him food because I had forbidden Jeannie to go.'

She wouldn't make any more excuses, but Jeannie did.

'Meg knew I was worried, Daddy,' she said. 'That's why she did it.'

Adam shook his head.

'That's not good enough,' he said. 'You must have known that what you were doing was irresponsible and asking for trouble. I can't understand how you—'

'Adam,' Meg broke in. 'Not now.'

All the colour had drained from Jeannie's face, and her

eyes were huge. She had tried valiantly not to cry, but now silent tears ran down her cheeks.

'I'm taking Jeannie back to bed,' Meg said. 'You can say all you want to later.'

Without giving him a chance to reply, she took the little girl's hand in hers and led her back upstairs to her room. It was a long time before she managed to get Jeannie calmed down, and she sat there until at last the child fell asleep. Then she went downstairs.

Adam swung round when she went in, angry words ready, but Meg got in first.

'I know what I did was wrong,' she said quickly, 'and I'm very sorry about that. But this is the worst possible thing for Jeannie—you and I talking to each other like this, and her dog out in the hills somewhere, hurt.'

He turned away from her.

'I cannot help what has happened,' he said, his voice low. 'The dog was found near sheep that had been killed, and Gavin Ferguson shot him.'

Meg put one hand on his arm.

'I know that, Adam,' she said, 'and so does Jeannie. But if you could only have supported her, said you didn't think her Glen could be a killer...'

His face was bleak, his eyes very dark. And very cold.

'And how could I be doing that, and the facts unable to be argued with?' he said, his voice dangerously quiet. 'And nothing you can say is any excuse for encouraging Jeannie in what she did. Not only encouraging her, but going there yourself. I had thought you to have more sense, Meg.'

Meg moved her hand from his arm.

'Sense doesn't always come into it, Adam,' she told him shakily. 'Sometimes other things are more important.'

She left him, and went to her room, looking in on Jeannie from time to time through what seemed like a very long night. Just as dawn was breaking she went through again.

There were tears on Jeannie's cheeks, although she was asleep, and Meg wiped them away gently before she turned to go back to her own room.

'How is she?' Adam said gruffly, from the doorway.

'She's asleep,' Meg told him, 'but she's been crying.'

He stood aside to let her pass, but when she went into her own room he was still standing there, looking at the sleeping child. Slowly, Meg's anger towards him faded. There was no other way he could have behaved in the circumstances, she thought reluctantly.

She wanted to say something to him, but her courage failed at the sight of the unyielding bleakness in the set of his dark head.

He left early, giving her a brief nod as he went out to the sheep, with Rex at his heels.

'Is Daddy still very angry?' Jeannie said when she woke up.

'I don't know,' Meg replied. 'I haven't seen him to speak to yet.' She took Jeannie's hands in hers. 'I understand how you feel, Jeannie, but your father is right—we did behave in an irresponsible way. We shouldn't have fed Glen.'

Jeannie pulled her hands away.

'I don't care what Daddy says. I just want Glen back!' Then, her defiance gone, she said shakily, 'And now he's out there in the hills, and he's hurt, and there's no one to look after him.'

Meg held her while she cried, desolate, heartbroken sobs that nearly broke Meg's own heart. She felt completely at a loss. This stress and upset was, as she'd said to Adam, the worst thing possible for Jeannie. But there was nothing she could do about it. Throughout the day she tried to take Jeannie's mind off the thought of the dog, but she could see it was no use. There had been no opportunity for her so far to go to the village and see Colin, but she assured

Jeannie that somehow the following day she would manage it.

That in the afternoon she heard Betsy open the door to the boy, and she ran downstairs.

'He's wanting to see Jeannie,' Betsy said, standing in the doorway, her plump arms folded, 'but I told him we're not to have any germs near Jeannie, like you said, Meg, and here he is just better from the cold.'

Meg looked at the boy doubtfully. Betsy was right, but—

'I'm fine now, Meg,' Colin assured her. He smiled engagingly, but his eyes were anxious.

'I think it would do Jeannie good to see Colin,' Meg said. 'He can stand right at the door, and not go near Jeannie. Just a quick visit, Colin.'

She took him upstairs. Jeannie was sitting up in bed, obviously listening.

'Have you heard about Glen?' she said passionately. 'They shot him, Colin.'

'I know,' Colin replied. 'My dad heard last night, and he told me.' He moved closer, and Meg put a restraining hand on his arm. 'I stayed off school this afternoon, Jeannie, and I came here to look for him. He's in the cave, right at the back, and—and his leg's hurt. He can't walk. I gave him food, and he let me stroke him, Jeannie, and...' He turned to Meg. 'He canna stay there, Meg, and him hurt.'

He was trying hard not to cry, and so was Jeannie. Meg herself felt her throat become tight.

'You know what Mr Ferguson said,' she reminded the children. And herself. 'He was seen near the sheep that had been killed.'

Colin shook his red head.

'He hadn't been at the sheep,' he said with certainty. 'There was no blood on his mouth or on his chest. I've seen a dog that's been at the sheep—he was my gran-dad's—and Glen hadn't touched them.'

'Maybe he was chasing away the dogs that really did it,' Jeannie suggested. She got out of bed purposefully. 'I'm going to see him.'

'You can't do that, Jeannie,' Meg told her, in a tone which, she hoped, would brook no argument. 'You're not well enough yet to walk that far. Quite apart from anything your father would have to say about it.'

The colour which had come into Jeannie's cheeks faded. Her anguished grey eyes, held Meg's, unwavering.

Meg gave in.

'All right, I'll go,' she said.

'I'll come with you,' Colin said eagerly, but she shook her head and said that he had better go home.

'You'll have some explaining to do about why you weren't at school,' she reminded him.

'Och, my mum won't bother,' he assured her. His face fell. 'But we were starting to make cards for Mother's Day, though. I'll just do mine fast next time we work on them, and, anyway, we've plenty time.'

He said goodbye to Jeannie, and promised her that he'd come back to find out about Glen and what they were to do. Meg went to the door with him, and then put on her anorak.

'Betsy,' she said, 'I'm going out for a little while. Just for a walk. Will you keep an eye on Jeannie? Maybe take a cup of tea up to her, and have your own with her.'

'She'll be very upset about the dog, I suppose,' Betsy said. 'It's a great pity she has the worry of that, and her not well, is it not?'

Meg agreed that it was a great pity—quite certain that Betsy knew very well what she was going to do. When she reached the door the old housekeeper said, 'He's never a sheep-killer, our Glen. I've known him all his life. He's a sheep-dog, not a sheep-killer.'

And I don't know him at all, but I'm accepting all these character references, Meg thought ruefully as she hurried along the path to the low foothills and on to the cave. She saw no one, and she was glad of that, glad that Betsy had mentioned that Adam was with the shepherd in the field beside the loch.

It was dark inside the cave, and she was glad that she had remembered to bring a torch with her. Slowly, quietly, she went deeper inside, saying the dog's name.

'Glen? Where are you, boy? Glen?'

There was a low warning growl, and she stopped. Now she could see him, lying right at the back of the cave. She went towards him with her hand out, saying his name softly. There were no more growls, and when she reached him, her hand still held out, she knelt down.

'Poor boy, then, poor Glen,' she murmured, and after what seemed an endless time he licked her hand. She patted his head, still speaking softly to him, and then she shone the torch on him. Colin was right. There was no blood on his muzzle and on his chest. But his leg was bleeding badly, and he whined when she touched it gently.

The only thing she had with her was a scarf, and she tied it around his leg, hoping that he wouldn't try to move. Even as she thought that, she realised that there was no way he could walk or move at all. If they trace him here, if they find him, he hasn't a chance, she thought, and with a spurt of strength, born of desperation, she tried to lift him. But he was a big dog, too heavy for her.

She patted him again, and stood up.

'I'm coming back, Glen,' she told the dog. 'I'm going to get help for you.' His topaz eyes were fixed trustingly on her face, and there was just the faintest movement of his tail.

She went out of the cave, her eyes blurred with tears, and back along the path towards the farm, knowing there was only one thing she could do.

She needed help with the dog, and there was only one person she could ask.

Adam.

CHAPTER EIGHT

ALL through the day the dark and threatening clouds had lain low on the hills, and now, as Meg ran down the path, a sudden squall of rain drove fiercely on her, soaking her in no time. She could barely see where the path forked to lead to the loch, and as she ran along the shore the grey water surged and swirled against the stony shore.

Where would Adam be?

She peered through the driving rain. Yes, there were the sheep, and Rex, and Adam, straightening now.

'Adam,' she called. He didn't hear, but she ran towards him. 'Adam!'

He turned, alarm on his face.

'Jeannie's all right—it isn't that,' Meg said quickly. Before she could lose her courage she said, 'Adam, I need your help.'

As suddenly as it had started, the rain stopped. The big farmer looked down at her.

'You're soaked, lassie,' he said. 'I'll just tell Jock I'm going.'

With the dog at his heels, he strode across to where the old shepherd was bending over a ewe and a lamb. As Meg watched, the lamb staggered to its feet and the old man straightened. Adam spoke to him, and then came back to Meg, leaving the dog with the shepherd.

'Now,' he said, and the momentary warmth in his voice had gone, 'what is it? What do you need me to do?'

Meg took a deep and steadying breath.

'Glen is in a cave, and he's hurt,' she said baldly. 'I tried to lift him, but he's too heavy for me.'

117

She heard Adam take an even deeper breath as he looked down at her.

'Are you out of your mind?' he said. 'Just what do you want me to do with him?'

Meg lifted her chin.

'I want you to bring him to the farm,' she said. 'I want to see how badly hurt he is, and...and then...'

Slowly the anger left Adam's face.

'And then what, Meg?' he asked her, so gently that the tightness in her throat made her able to do no more than shake her head wordlessly. 'I cannot do that, and half the farmers in the glen after him for sheep-killing.'

Now Meg found her voice.

'There is no blood on his muzzle or on his chest,' she said clearly. 'And there would be if he had just killed sheep. I know that because Colin Cameron told me.'

'Is that laddie in on this too?'

Meg put her hand on his arm.

'Adam, Jeannie is desperately worried about Glen. I don't care how unprofessional and unscientific this sounds, but if we don't do something about the dog she's much less likely to get better. I know that. And...'

She looked up at him.

'You can't leave him to die there, alone, starving,' she said. 'You have to do something. Not just for Jeannie, for the dog himself.'

For an eternity, it seemed, he stood there, his dark eyes on her face. Then he sighed.

'You're right, I can't leave him there,' he said.

He turned and strode back along the path, so fast that Meg could barely keep up with him. When they reached the fork in the path he slowed.

'We should wait until it's dark,' he said, 'although with the clouds so low we're not likely to be seen. We'll take a chance.'

When they turned off the path towards the cave Meg led the way.

'He's in here,' she told Adam, and she took out her torch. 'Look.'

She shone the torch down on the dog. He lifted his head, and even in the torchlight Meg could see the look in his eyes as he recognised Adam.

The big man knelt beside the dog, and now there was no doubt about Glen knowing that this was his master. He whined, and tried to get up.

'There, boy, easy,' Adam said. He took the dog's head between his hands, and looked at him. 'You're right, Meg,' he said. 'There is no blood from any killing. All right, boy, we'll take you home.'

He lifted the dog in his arms. Meg tightened the make-shift bandage she had put on Glen's leg, and they set off down the path to the farm. It was raining again, and that was a good thing, Meg thought, for they were less likely to be seen if there should be anyone around.

The kitchen was warm, and the light already on, when they reached the farm.

'Mercy on us,' Betsy exclaimed. 'The puir dog!'

'Bring his basket in, Betsy, and find an old blanket,' Adam said.

Meg was already preparing hot water and a bowl to wash the dog's wound. Adam, with the dog still in his arms, opened the door to the hall and called, 'Jeannie, put on your dressing-gown and come down.'

Betsy came back with the dog's basket with a blanket in it. Gently, Adam put the collie down, and Meg knelt beside him.

'Glen, oh, Glen!'

Jeannie flew across the room, and in a moment her arms were around the dog.

'Is he badly hurt, Daddy?' she asked, her voice muffled against the collie's coat.

'I don't know, lass,' Adam replied. 'Let Meg bathe his wound, and we'll see.'

Meg took her scarf off the dog's leg, and began to clean away the blood. Adam and Jeannie and Betsy watched her, and the dog's golden eyes rested on her face, full of trust.

'The bullet must have passed right through,' she said at last. 'It's a flesh wound, and I don't think it's done any lasting damage. It doesn't even need to be stitched, just time to heal.'

'Just as well,' Adam said, 'for we could not be asking the vet to come and see him, could we?'

Jeannie's eyes met Meg's, with the unspoken shared thought. Adam had made himself part of this, not only with bringing Glen to the farm but with his words.

'I think,' he said carefully, 'we had better have his basket in your room, Jeannie, where he will not be seen.'

Meg carried the basket upstairs, and Adam carried the dog. Jeannie needed no persuading to go back to bed.

'Betsy's bringing him some food,' she said, 'and I'll see that he eats every bit of it. What about when he needs to go out, Daddy?'

'Well, now, it looks as if I'll have to be carrying him out and in for a bit,' Adam said. He shook his head. 'It's a terrible thing when a man gets into the hands of bossy women. Meg, telling me I had to go the cave and bring Glen to the farm, and now you!'

Jeannie looked up at him.

'Come here, Daddy,' she said imperiously.

Her father sat on the side of the bed, and she hugged him.

'You're the best daddy in the whole world,' she told him passionately. She held out her arms to Meg. 'And you're the best Meg.'

It wasn't going to be easy, Meg knew. There could be all sorts of problems. The first arose when Jock, the shepherd, brought Rex back. Rex walked around the kitchen, stiff-legged, sniffing suspiciously. The best thing to do, Adam said when the shepherd had gone, was to let Rex and Glen meet. Which could be a chancy thing, he admitted, but better to have it happen under supervision.

Certainly there was one bad moment when Rex growled and his lips curled back from his teeth at the sight of the other dog in his basket in Jeannie's room. But Glen stayed very still, other than making an attempt to roll over on his back. After a moment Rex went over to him and sniffed him. Then, apparently satisfied, he turned and went back down to the kitchen.

'Glen did his best to show Rex that he accepts that Rex is the boss dog,' Adam told Meg and Jeannie. 'They'll be fine now, the two of them.'

Later, when Meg and Adam were alone in the kitchen, it was clear that in spite of being boss dog Rex was quite happy to do without the basket and settle for a blanket on the rug beside the warm stove. Meg, smiling at the sight, turned to find Adam watching her. Although he was clearly no longer angry, his lean dark face was sombre.

'Are you sorry we brought Glen back to the farm, Adam?' she asked, taking the bull by the horns.

He shook his head.

'No, Meg, I could not be sorry, and Jeannie with a light in her eyes that I will never forget when she saw him. And you were right, I could not be leaving my dog hurt and alone the way he was. But I am thinking that there could be a great deal of trouble ahead for all of us.'

Meg knew all too well what he meant for she had thought of it all herself. What if someone saw Glen here, and the others farmers found out? She didn't know, but there could well be the threat of police action. If not, at the very least

Adam would be decidedly unpopular with the other farmers. And when Glen was better—

'Even if we get through this next wee while, what about when he is better?' Adam said, echoing her thoughts. 'We cannot keep him hidden for the rest of his life, Meg.'

'I know that,' Meg replied. She could not—she dared not—say it, but she couldn't help thinking it. *If we can only keep him for a while—for Jeannie. For as long as Jeannie needs him to be there.*

With an effort, Adam smiled.

'Anyway, we will just have to do the best we can, now that we have landed ourselves in this.' He looked down at her. 'You look fair worn out, Meg, and no wonder.'

She managed to return his smile, although she felt her own smile was more than a little tremulous.

'I think I feel just what you said—fair worn out, Adam.'

They went upstairs together, and looked into Jeannie's room. Glen was asleep in his basket beside Jeannie's bed, but he was instantly alert, with a low growl that was immediately followed by an apologetic wag of his long, feathery tail. Adam bent and patted him.

'I'll not bother you now, boy, but I'll be in early in the morning to take you down to the farmyard.' He fondled the dog's ears, and his voice was less than steady. 'And I'd stand up in any court and swear you're no sheep-killer, Glen.'

They went out of the room together, and Adam closed the door softly. In the dimly lit hall Meg looked up at him.

'You're a nice man, Adam Kerr,' she told him.

This time his smile was real and warm.

'I think perhaps that is high praise you are giving me, Meg, is it not?'

Meg was all at once very conscious of his nearness to her in the dim light of the hall.

'I think perhaps it is,' she agreed, her voice very low.

'Meg,' he said. 'Oh, Meg, lass.' And then he said something else, words that she didn't understand.

'What did you say, Adam?' she asked him.

'Just words in the Gaelic. Some day, perhaps, I will tell you the meaning.'

For an endless time, it seemed to her, he stood there close to her, and the only sound she could hear was the uneven thudding of her heart. She didn't know whether he moved first or whether she moved first but with a rightness that seemed inevitable his arms were around her, holding her close to him, and his lips found hers in an urgent and demanding kiss that brought an immediate response throughout her whole body.

Afterwards, she knew very well that it had only been the thought of the sleeping child in the room beside them which had made them draw apart, slowly, reluctantly.

Adam looked down at her, and she wondered if he knew how desperately she longed to go back into his arms.

'This is not the time or the place, Meg, lass,' he said unsteadily. 'And also...' He stopped. 'I think you had better go to your room, and I will go to mine.' Gently, he touched her cheek, and then, with one finger, traced the outline of her mouth, still warm from his kiss. 'Goodnight, Meg.'

'Goodnight, Adam,' she murmured, and she did as he'd said, and went to her bedroom.

It was a long time before she fell asleep, and when she did her dreams were a bewildering confusion of so many things that had happened in that day. Colin and his news of the dog. Jeannie's distressed plea for Meg's help. That first sight of the wounded dog in the cave, and her headlong rush to Adam. Adam, carrying Glen to the farm through the driving rain. Jeannie's face, candle-lit with joy, at the sight of her beloved dog. The rough tenderness in Adam's voice as he'd spoken to Glen.

And the passionate demand of his lips on hers, of his arms around her, his body close to hers.

Her cheeks were warm with the memory of that kiss when she woke to hear Jeannie's voice and Adam's, coming from Jeannie's room. Hastily Meg pulled on her dressing-gown and went through. Adam was just putting Glen back in his basket, and Jeannie was sitting up in bed, her cheeks flushed, her eyes bright.

'Daddy took Glen outside, Meg, and he's much better already,' she said excitedly. The dog wagged his tail, confirming this.

'He tried to stand up,' Adam told her. 'The sore leg gave way, but he did try. It looks as if you might need to clean him up a bit again, though.'

Meg knelt to look at the dog's dressing, relieved to see that the wound had, in fact, bled very little.

'I think we'll leave him,' she said. 'I'll have a look later.'

Jeannie decided to come down to the kitchen for breakfast, and Meg wondered if Adam was as relieved as she was to have the little girl with them so that there was no opportunity for any reference to the previous night.

'What will we do when Dr Macrae or Dr Neil comes to see me?' Jeannie asked chattily.

Adam's eyes met Meg's in shared dismay. That was something they hadn't thought of or planned for.

Meg thought quickly.

'You'll have to come down here, Jeannie,' she said. She looked at the little girl's bright face. 'You look well enough for that.'

'I am well enough,' Jeannie said decisively. 'And I want to ask when I can go back to school. Colin says they're making—' She broke off. 'Colin says they're doing nice things when they have art.'

Adam stood.

'We'll have to see about that,' he said. 'I'm off out to

the sheep. No, Rex, you're not going upstairs to see how your friend is. You can pay him a visit later, maybe.'

The door closed behind him. Just what did I expect him to do? Meg asked herself, stifling a strong feeling of disappointment. A shared glance—a brush of the hand? Yes, she thought, that would have done.

I am not brooding over this, she told herself severely. Adam was right last night when he said that this was not the time or the place. Not when we don't know what we're going to do about Glen. And when there's so much unknown about Jeannie.

'We'll have to let Colin know about Glen,' Jeannie said, when Meg took her back up to her room.

Meg herself didn't see that as a priority, but Jeannie pointed out that Colin might go back to the cave to see how Glen was, and someone might see him.

'So we do have to tell him,' she insisted.

Meg smiled, glad to see the little girl so bright.

'I think your daddy is right. You're becoming bossy,' she said.

'Maybe I'm learning it from someone,' Jeannie replied almost cheekily. I shouldn't build too much on this, Meg told herself, but maybe, just maybe, the combination of the drug therapy and this boost to Jeannie could bring about the miracle they needed.

If she went to the village around lunchtime she could catch Colin then, she thought. Betsy was glad to be left in charge, and she promised that if either of the doctors came she would call for Jeannie to come down.

'I'll not let anyone set a foot in the room where Glen is,' she said fiercely.

At the door, Meg turned.

'When is it you have an appointment with Dr Macrae, Betsy?' she asked.

'Tomorrow,' the old housekeeper said, 'but I was thinking—'

'Oh, no,' Meg told her very firmly. 'You're going to keep that appointment, Betsy.'

The school bell rang as she got out of the car, and very soon she saw the small red-headed boy alone, scuffing his shoes as he walked across the playground.

'Colin,' she called, and his face brightened when he looked up and saw her. She told him that she and Adam had got Glen to the house, and that his leg was going to be all right.

'But no one must know that he's there,' she said, and Colin nodded.

'It's like he's a secret agent in a safe house,' he said eagerly, and in spite of the seriousness of it all Meg had to struggle to keep her face straight as she agreed that, yes, it was something like that. Colin asked if he could come and see Jeannie, and Meg said that he could.

She was more than a little worried when she left him, just because of one more person knowing, but there was nothing more to be done other than to impress on Colin the need for secrecy and silence.

Since Jeannie had become ill, there had been no possibility of her going to John Drummond, to do his exercises with him. She looked at her watch. A quarter of an hour wouldn't bother Betsy, she was sure.

The district nurse herself was just leaving the house when Meg arrived, and her face lit up.

'I've been doing the best I could with the exercises you showed me,' she said, 'but it's often late when I get back, and John is tired by then.' Her eyes were shadowed. 'He's been a bit low this past week. I know it happens with MS, but I find the depression harder to cope with than the physical problems.'

Meg knew very well, and Beth herself would know, that

the break in the regularity of the exercise programme certainly wouldn't have helped John. Because she knew that, she wasn't surprised to be greeted with hostility when she went in.

'Managed to find a few minutes for me, have you?' John asked her.

'I'm sorry about the break, but it was unavoidable,' Meg said equably. She sat down beside him, and began the stretch, hold, and relax routine, first with one arm, then the other, to combat the muscle spasticity.

When she felt that he was tiring she stopped as it was important not to let him overtire himself in any way.

'I'll try to come back soon, John,' she said, 'but I can't promise.' She hesitated, and then said levelly that little Jeannie was far from well.

After a moment John nodded, accepting that she wouldn't say any more. Awkwardly, he said, 'I know you would come if you could, Meg. I'm sorry about the wee lassie.'

Perhaps I'll look into the surgery on the way back to the farm, Meg thought as she got into the car. Just as she was about to start the engine another car drew up beside her, a sleek sports car which she recognised, her heart sinking, in the same moment that she recognised its driver.

Helen Ferguson wound down the window.

'Hello,' she said, pleasantly. 'It's…Meg, isn't it?'

She pushed the shining fall of blonde hair back from her face, a face so perfect that once again Meg was all too conscious of her hastily applied lipstick and her lack of any eye make-up.

'I'm so glad to hear Jeannie is much better,' Helen said. 'I'll be ringing Adam, of course, but you might tell him I'm here for the weekend.'

'I'll do that,' Meg replied, equally pleasantly she hoped.

'You can tell him, too,' Helen said, 'that we can make up for lost time now.'

With a dazzling smile, she drove off.

CHAPTER NINE

MAKE up for lost time indeed, Meg thought indignantly as she watched the glamorous Helen drive away. What does she think Adam has been doing, and Jeannie so ill?

In fairness, of course, she reminded herself, Helen didn't know the truth about Jeannie's illness, but somehow Meg didn't think that would make a great deal of difference. Helen would still think that time spent away from her was time lost.

She was a little surprised at her own immediate knee-jerk reaction to the blonde woman. She had always prided herself on not being a hasty judge of character. Here I am, Meg thought, more than a little ashamed of herself, not even giving her the benefit of any doubt at all!

And that wasn't the only thought she was a little ashamed of. As she drove down through the village to the surgery she couldn't help wondering what Helen would have thought if she had seen two people in each other's arms last night on the landing at Craigrannoch.

Neil had just seen his last patient when Meg arrived at the surgery. It was old Andrew, the ulcer patient, and he gave Meg a cheerful wave as he walked away from the surgery, headed, Meg couldn't help thinking, for the pub at the hotel to be ready for opening time.

She said as much to Neil, and he nodded.

'I've been reading the riot act to him again, but he thinks he knows best.'

He looked at her, his blue eyes so searching that Meg felt her cheeks grow warm.

'You look as if you've been having quite a time, Nurse

Bennett,' he said, only half teasing her. 'You have dark shadows under your eyes. I thought Jeannie was making good progress.'

'She is,' Meg assured him, all too well aware that she couldn't say anything about the ongoing worry about Glen and the need to keep his presence hidden. 'Just a few things happening all at once,' she said vaguely.

'You need to be taken out of yourself,' the young doctor said. 'I prescribe something completely different—come with me to the ceilidh next week.' He held up one hand. 'I know—you're going to ask me what a ceilidh is. Well, now, let me see if I can be describing a ceilidh to you. It's a cross between a party and a dance and a rave. There's music, there's food, there's dancing, there's singing. It's the father and mother of all the parties you've ever been to in your life. Everyone in the glen will be there. It will do you the world of good. Oh, yes, and it takes place in the school hall.'

Meg had to smile at his enthusiasm.

'Everyone in the glen will be there?' she said. 'I'd better see what Adam thinks—maybe he'll want us to take Jeannie. If it would do me good I'm sure it would do Jeannie good too. Can I let you know, Neil?'

'Sure,' Neil said immediately, but there was something about the questioning look in his blue eyes that made Meg distinctly uncomfortable. Hastily, she said she would have to go. He came out to the car with her.

'We've missed you, Meg,' he said, serious now. 'Quite apart from the help you are to Uncle Jim, and myself, and to Beth.'

It's just Neil's way, Meg told herself as she drove back to the farm. I'm probably the only unmarried young female in the glen—apart from Helen, of course. But she didn't think that a hard-up young doctor who planned on returning to the Sudan would be of much interest to Helen Ferguson.

She gave Adam Helen's message when he came in that evening.

'She's here for the weekend, and she'll be in touch,' she told him. 'And she said to tell you that now you can make up for lost time.'

She didn't know what reaction she'd expected from Adam, but all he did was nod and go on reading the *Farmers' Weekly* which had come in with the day's mail.

The next morning was Betsy's appointment with Dr Macrae.

'I can take her, Adam,' Meg said, when she and Adam talked about it at breakfast. 'Jeannie is well enough to come with me. She and I can stay in the car while Betsy is with Dr Macrae.' Because it wouldn't be a good idea to let Jeannie go into the waiting-room, where she might be close to people with all sorts of germs. She didn't have to say it, she knew, as Adam's eyes met hers. Jeannie, having breakfast in the kitchen now, turned from her father to Meg.

'I could see Colin at playtime,' she said eagerly.

Adam shook his head.

'I don't think so, Jeannie,' he said. 'And I'm sure Meg agrees with me.'

Jeannie's face fell, then she was distracted by another thought. Would Glen be all right in the house alone? she asked. What if someone came, and he barked?

'It's a chance we'll have to take,' Adam said, thinking about this. 'I'll try to look in and see that he's all right. But it isn't very likely that anyone will come.'

'If it's the postie he would think it was Rex,' Jeannie said, 'having a day off from working with the sheep.'

She giggled at her little joke, and once again Meg found Adam's eyes meeting hers, this time in the shared joy of seeing how bright the little girl was.

Betsy's appointment had been arranged at the start of the

old doctor's consulting time. Meg took her in, and then went back to sit in the car with Jeannie. Half an hour later Betsy came out, her cheeks pink, holding a bottle of pills.

'Dr Macrae says you did the right thing, getting me to go and see him, Meg,' she said, settling herself in the front passenger seat. 'He had a fancy name for it, but it's my blood pressure too high.'

'Hypertension,' Meg suggested, for this was what she'd suspected when she'd asked Betsy about her different symptoms.

'Aye, that will be it,' Betsy agreed. She handed Meg a note. 'I'm to take these wee white pills, and Dr Macrae says he wants this blood pressure checked after a few days of the wee white pills, and would you pick up some instrument from the surgery?'

'A baumanometer,' Meg said. 'Good, then I can check it without you having to go to the surgery.'

'It will be to save me the trouble of going,' Betsy said, but Meg knew there was a more valid reason. She would have a more true reading of the old woman's blood pressure under normal conditions as the very fact of going to the surgery could well raise it.

A quick look at Dr Macrae's note told her that Betsy's blood pressure was 170 over 100, and that diastolic figure would certainly have to be watched.

Jeannie was none the worse for her short outing, and there was a note from Adam on the kitchen table to say that he had looked in and Glen was fine.

Which the dog certainly was. With each day he was moving more easily. The wounded leg was still very stiff, and obviously causing him pain, but now when Adam carried him down to the farmyard in the early morning and at dusk he could manage to hobble a few steps.

'And soon,' Adam said to Meg, the next night, as they stood together, watching Jeannie and the dog, Jeannie clapping her hands in delight when Glen managed to walk a little, 'we will be having to think about what we are to do for when that leg is completely better there's no way we can be keeping Glen in Jeannie's bedroom.'

'I know that,' Meg agreed. 'Adam, look at Rex—you would almost think he wants to help Glen.'

The younger collie was walking along beside Glen, and when the wounded dog gave up and lay down Rex lay down, too, his nose on his paws, his eyes—a darker golden than Glen's—anxious.

'Aye, it's a beautiful friendship,' Adam said soberly, 'and a fine thing to see, but I wish we could think of a way out of this. Anyway, that's Glen for the day. I'll take him back upstairs.'

With Glen settled back in his basket, and Jeannie dressed in a tracksuit, sighing deeply because Adam and Meg said she couldn't go to school yet, Adam lifted his jacket from the coatrack at the back door, ready to go out.

'I met Beth Drummond yesterday, Meg,' he said. 'She was saying how much John was benefiting from the exercises you had been doing with him. Why don't you take a wee while today and drive up to the village? Jeannie's fine with Betsy and Glen for company, are you not, lass?'

Jeannie nodded.

'Yes, but I'm awful bored, Daddy. And Colin says they're doing such interesting things at school.'

'No school till the check-up, Jeannie,' Meg said firmly. 'You know that.'

Adam's dark eyes met hers. The check-up in Inverness would tell them whether this could be regarded as a successful remission. Meg herself couldn't help feeling very positive about this, going on nothing more scientific than the way Jeannie looked and behaved, but the blood test would tell if her feeling was valid or not.

John's welcome was casual, but when Meg had finished

doing the usual exercises with him he asked her if she had noticed an increased lack of co-ordination in his hands and his wrists.

'Yes, I did notice, John,' Meg said, for there was no use being less than honest. 'I was just going to mention to you that we can try weighted bracelets or perhaps wrist cuffs. I'll talk to Dr Macrae about it.'

With difficulty, John got up and walked to the door with her.

'Try walking with your feet wider apart, John,' Meg suggested. 'Even when you're using your cane, that will increase your walking stability.'

When she left him, promising to come back as soon as she could, she drove to the surgery at the far end of the village so that she could talk to Dr Macrae about getting the devices John Drummond needed.

The old doctor was out, and Neil made a note of what Meg wanted.

'I could have done with your help for surgery,' he said. 'Full house, and Uncle Jim and Beth both away. Old Mrs Farquhar has had a heart attack. They're stabilising her and they'll be there till the ambulance comes. Time for coffee?'

Before Meg could reply, the phone rang. Watching the young doctor, she could see immediately that this was a crisis.

'Don't worry, I'll be there right away,' he said crisply. He put down the telephone, and turned to Meg.

'Jean Campbell,' he told her, picking up his bag and reaching for his coat. 'She's only due in a fortnight, but she's gone into labour. Uncle Jim saw her a couple of days ago, and the baby's breech.' He hesitated. 'I could use some help, Meg.'

Meg had already thought about what she could do. She phoned the farm and told Betsy what had happened. The old housekeeper said immediately that, of course, Meg was to go with the doctor.

On the way along the high street Neil told her that Dr Macrae had decided he would send Jean to Inverness to have her baby as it was breech.

'And this is her third so we won't have much time,' he said, as they reached the cottage and saw the young woman's neighbour, looking out anxiously.

'Hurry, Doctor, I think you'll just be in time,' she told them.

Jean was lying on the bed, her eyes dark with pain, her forehead damp. There was no time to examine her, only time for Neil and Meg to open the sterile packs of gloves and get ready to deliver. Already one tiny foot had appeared, and then another, and now the contractions were fast and intense.

'Good girl. Stop pushing, Jean,' Neil said, and he grasped the little legs and helped the tiny body to ease out. The shoulders followed, and suddenly he was holding a red-faced baby girl. There was one heart-stopping moment of silence, and then the baby gave a loud and outraged yell.

'Blanket, Meg,' Neil said, and Meg handed him the blanket which Jean's neighbour had hurriedly got ready. Expertly, he wrapped the baby in the blanket.

'Pretty good, Neil,' Meg said. 'I can see you've had plenty of practice, delivering babies, in the Sudan.'

Too much, the young doctor assured her. 'And usually as quick as this. What is it, Meg?'

Meg, in response to an instinct that she had learned not to question, turned back to the young woman on the bed.

'I think—I think there's another baby,' she said, startled. The contractions had stopped, but if she was right there would no time to spare when they started again.

'You had a scan, didn't you, Jean?' Neil asked, examining the woman on the bed. 'Babies can be sneaky, of course, one hiding behind the other... You're right, Meg. Here we go.'

The second baby's head crowned as he spoke.

'Yours, I think,' Neil said, and he stepped aside, letting Meg take his place.

There was no time to think for with the next push the baby's shoulders slithered out.

'One more push, Jean,' Meg said, glad that she'd had a couple of months on Maternity not too long ago. 'That's it. I've got him.'

The next moment she was holding a baby boy. Neil was holding the first twin, the young mother was laughing and crying at the same time and Mrs Sorley, the neighbour, was standing at the door, saying over and over again, 'Mercy on us, twins! Mercy on us! And here's the kettle boiling, and no time for it to be needed.'

'It's needed now,' Neil told her. 'You can make a pot of nice strong tea for us all!'

A little while later, with both babies cleaned and wrapped up, one on each side of the smiling young mother, all four of them drank the babies' health in that good strong tea.

'It's something you never get used to,' Neil said, when he and Meg got back to the surgery. 'That thrill of delivering a baby. I love it.'

'So do I,' Meg agreed. 'And twins. You delivered the breech one perfectly, Neil. I know how difficult it can be. Look at the time—I'd better get back to the farm.'

'And I'd better let Uncle Jim know that he has two new patients on his list,' Neil said. Taking her by surprise, he kissed her cheek. 'Thanks for your help, Meg. I'll be in to see Jeannie soon.'

Meg drove back to the farm, unable to stop smiling. She was still carrying the glow of the birth when she and Jeannie, playing cards in Jeannie's room, heard Adam's Land Rover draw up at the back door.

'Daddy's back early,' Jeannie said, and a few minutes later Adam came into her room, Colin Cameron with him.

'I met this young man on his bike,' Adam said, 'heading here, so I gave him a lift.'

Colin was kneeling down beside Glen's basket, patting the dog, but for once there was more than her beloved dog on Jeannie's mind.

'Do you know what, Daddy?' she said excitedly. 'Meg helped Dr Neil to deliver Mrs Campbell's baby, and it wasn't just one—it was twins!'

'So I heard in the village,' Adam said, and he smiled. 'I think everyone knows about the unexpected twins, and you and Neil just in time to deliver them.'

'Isn't that exciting, Colin?' Jeannie said.

The boy shrugged. 'What's so special about twins?' he asked. 'Dogs and cats have them all the time!'

Meg couldn't help smiling, and Adam's dark eyes met hers as he smiled too. The shared closeness of their amusement was something Meg found herself holding onto in the next few days—because, more and more, she became certain that Adam was avoiding any possibility of being alone with her.

Yet it was only right and natural, she told herself reasonably, that he should want to spend the evenings, keeping Jeannie company, either in her room or in the kitchen. And very pleasant evenings they were, too, with the three of them playing Scrabble or Monopoly or some of the many card games Adam and Jeannie had played in their months away from the farm. Later, when Jeannie was in bed, Meg would sit on the couch beside the fire, but it seemed that Adam always had some work to do, something that took him out of the room—away from her.

What would he do, she wondered, in a few days when they went to Inverness for Jeannie's check-up, and they were thrown into each other's company?

On the day before Jeannie's appointment Adam had just come in from checking the sheep, and was sitting down, taking off his boots, when they heard a car draw up outside.

'Quick, Jeannie, take Glen upstairs,' Adam said, for the dog was now spending a good part of each day in the kitchen, always being hurried out of sight if there was any danger of him being seen.

'I'll stay with him, Daddy,' Jeannie said, from the door. 'I think it's Helen.'

A moment later Adam opened the door to Helen Ferguson. For once, Meg thought, ridiculously pleased, I'm just a little smarter than she usually finds me. She'd made a quick visit to John Drummond that afternoon and had got caught in rain so she'd washed her hair when she'd got back to the farm. For some reason, which she preferred not to go into too deeply, instead of just letting her brown curls dry she had hurried the process by blowdrying her hair, with Jeannie watching every step. Then, because her hair had looked really nice, some eye make-up had seemed a good idea, with the green eyeshadow perfectly matching the thick jersey she was wearing. This again was watched with breathless interest by Jeannie.

Now the faintest raising of Helen's eyebrows gave Meg the satisfaction of knowing that this was not unnoticed.

'You didn't return my call, Adam,' Helen said, sitting in the chair beside Adam's, 'and now I have to get back to the shop. What about having dinner with me next time you're in Inverness?'

To Meg's surprise, Adam said nothing about going there the next day, and she was glad that Jeannie was upstairs with the dog for surely the little girl would have mentioned it.

'But I'm coming for the ceilidh next weekend,' Helen said. She laughed. 'Not that ceilidhs are really my scene, but Mum and Dad feel we should put in an appearance.'

'I'd say your folks always seem to enjoy a good ceilidh, Helen,' Adam remarked. He turned to Meg. 'You'll not have been to a ceilidh, Meg. Jeannie's keen to go—we'll see how she is next week, and maybe we'll all go.'

Helen then spoke about the dinner-dance she had wanted Adam to go to, and mentioned people they both obviously knew. Meg, uncomfortable, was on the point of excusing herself and going upstairs to keep Jeannie company when Helen said, 'Oh, by the way, Adam, Dad asked me to tell you something rather unpleasant. That dog of yours—the one he managed to get a shot at—seems to have recovered, and he's been killing sheep again. Not on our farm this time, but Robert Barr found two of his sheep dead this morning.'

Adam stood up.

'He found them this morning?' he said, his voice tight.

Helen nodded. 'Dad and Robert Barr are getting together. They're determined to find the dog now.'

Adam's eyes met Meg's. He smiled, and the distance between them, of which Meg had been conscious, was gone.

'Just a minute,' he said, and he strode out of the room to the telephone in the hall. Helen, obviously thrown by his reaction, turned to Meg, but Meg, not caring whether she was being rude or not, put up one hand so that she could hear what Adam was saying.

'Gavin? Would you come over to Craigrannoch? Yes, right now. There's something I'd like you to see.'

At first, Helen was amused. 'What on earth does Adam think he's doing, getting my father—and Robert Barr, too—to come here?' she said to Meg, when they heard Adam speaking to the other farmer.

'We'd better wait and see, hadn't we?' Meg replied equably.

Adam came back into the room.

'They'll both be here soon,' he said.

Helen looked up at him.

'Are you going to throw your weight around about this, Adam?' she said, and she smiled. 'I like to see a man taking charge, but I have to warn you you'll be up against two very angry farmers.'

Adam smiled too.

'I'm sure you'll be right, Helen,' he said amiably. 'Would you like some more tea? I think Betsy's off, watching one of her favourite programmes, but Meg would make us some, would you not, Meg?'

'Certainly,' Meg said. She was enjoying this as much as Adam was. 'Or would you rather have coffee, Helen?'

Some of Helen's amusement began to fade. 'No, thanks,' she said, quite sharply.

'You don't have to wait, of course,' Adam told her, but she assured him that she was quite happy to wait.

'Adam,' Meg said, 'are you going to tell Jeannie?'

She wasn't sure quite what Adam had in mind, but it would surely involve Jeannie. And Glen.

Adam shook his head.

'I don't think so,' he said. 'We'll not bother her at the moment.'

He turned to Helen, and began to ask about her antique shop. Somewhat to Meg's surprise, he was surprisingly knowledgeable about Georgian silver, and talked for some time about a pair of candlesticks he had seen in Helen's shop. However, it was very clear to Meg that Helen's patience was wearing thin after a prolonged conversation about this.

At last there was the sound of a car, stopping outside, and very soon after the sound of another. Adam went to the door.

'Gavin—Robert,' he greeted the two men. Courteously, he introduced Robert Barr to Meg.

'My wife met you at the surgery the other week,' the big grey-haired man said, 'when she was in for the flu injection.' He turned to Adam. 'What's all this, Adam? I'm right sorry about the dog, but there's nothing else we can do but get out after him. Gavin thought he'd got him a week ago, but obviously the dog recovered.'

'Would you come with me?' Adam said. 'You can come too, Helen, if you like.'

Meg didn't wait to be asked—she didn't want to miss a minute of this. The two farmers, obviously thrown by being taken upstairs, followed Adam to Jeannie's door.

Adam opened it.

Jeannie was sitting up in bed, wide-eyed, and Glen was in his basket beside her. He lifted his head, alert, but he made no sound.

'There is your sheep-killer,' Adam said quietly. He pointed to the bandage on the dog's leg. 'And he's been here since you shot him a week ago, Gavin, unable to get out of this room unless I carried him.'

There was complete silence in the room for what seemed an endless time.

'Daddy?' Jeannie said at last, bewildered.

Adam went over to her.

'It's all right, lass,' he said, and his voice was gentle now. He sat on the side of the bed and patted the dog's head. 'There's been more sheep killed last night. I wanted Mr Ferguson and Mr Barr to come here so that they could see that, whatever dog did it, it wasn't our Glen.'

He stood up.

'Are you satisfied, Gavin? And you, Robert? I carried the dog here myself from the cave where he was lying, wounded, and he has been at Jeannie's side since then, and him still hardly able to do more than hobble a few steps.'

It was Gavin who recovered first.

'Jeannie, lass,' he said, awkwardly, 'I'm right glad about

this. I'm sorry I shot him, but perhaps it's for the best since that is what has proved that he is innocent.'

The other farmer nodded.

'There's no doubt about that,' he agreed, 'but we still have a dog out there somewhere, killing our sheep, Gavin, and we'll have to catch him.'

He held out his hand to Adam.

'No hard feelings, I hope, Adam?'

'None at all,' Adam said, and the three farmers shook hands. They went downstairs, and at the door, he said, 'As soon as Glen's leg is better I'll be using him for the sheep again. I think he and Rex will work fine together.'

He took Helen's brown suede jacket from the coat rack and held it out to her. There were two high spots of colour on Helen's cheeks, Meg noticed, and she didn't look too pleased at being ushered out along with her father and the other farmer.

When the door had closed behind them Adam turned to Meg.

'Was that not a grand thing?' he said, and the warmth of his smile made her see, suddenly, the boy he must have been. 'To have Glen's name cleared like that?'

'And you enjoyed every minute of it,' Meg said, smiling as well.

Impulsively, she stood on tiptoe and hugged him. He held her close to him, and just for a moment his lips brushed hers.

'Daddy, Meg—come and see,' Jeannie called excitedly from the top of the stairs. With a reluctance, which Meg could see Adam felt as much as she did, they drew apart and went out into the hall.

Glen, his bandaged leg stiff and awkward, was coming down the stairs slowly, carefully, encouraged by Jeannie beside him and Rex at the foot of the stairs, wagging his tail.

'There will be no holding him back now,' Adam said, 'and it will make it easier for Betsy when we are away in Inverness.'

There was no doubt, Meg thought the next day as they set off that it was easier for Jeannie to leave Glen now that he was in the clear, and now that he didn't have to be kept hidden.

'When we come back,' Jeannie said determinedly, 'I'll be going to school, and I'll be so glad not to have to worry about Glen. Betsy said she would phone Colin and tell him. He'll be pleased, too.'

Dear Jeannie, Meg thought with a catch in her throat, I do so hope that you're right—that you will be going to school.

The initial blood tests looked good, Dr Robinson told them around lunchtime. They would be rechecked, but the sedimentation level was good and the blood count acceptable.

'I'm afraid we have to do another of the nasty ones, Jeannie,' he said. 'You're very brave about that, I know.'

'I still don't jump for joy,' Jeannie assured him. 'Can Meg stay with me, like she did last time?'

Again Meg could almost feel Jeannie's pain when the stylet was removed and the small volume of bone and marrow aspirated. Jeannie had been sedated for this, and she was drowsy when it was over. Adam and Meg waited until she was asleep, and then left the hospital.

'Tomorrow morning we will know the best or the worst,' Adam said, his voice low. He went on, carefully, 'At least for now. And if the news is good that will be enough for me. One day at a time, and be grateful for that, one of the doctors in America said to me.'

He started the Land Rover, and turned to her.

'I forgot to tell you, Meg, Elspeth Ritchie has a group

of German tourists, and all her rooms are full. I've booked us in at the Castle Hotel—it's a small one.'

Meg had thought of them being in the pleasant and friendly bed and breakfast house, and she couldn't help feeling a little disappointed, but the hotel was, as Adam had said, small, and the receptionist, with her soft Highland accent, was as welcoming as Elspeth Ritchie had been. The porter took them up one floor to adjoining rooms, and Adam handed Meg the small overnight bag she had brought.

'Do you mind if we just have something to eat here at the hotel, Meg?' Adam asked her. 'There are fancy places in Inverness now, but I know the food here is good.'

Meg assured him that she didn't mind and later, when the waiter had cleared away their plates, with only the bones of their grilled salmon steaks left, she said that she didn't think he could have made a better choice.

'I should be taking you out to show you around Inverness, Meg,' Adam said, when they'd finished their coffee. 'Let's get our coats, and we'll have a look at the river and the castle and the old town.'

It was dusk—the gloaming, Meg was learning to call it—but when Adam stopped up on Castlehill the moon was rising.

'I always think it is a breath-taking view,' Adam said. 'Look, there is the Beauly Firth, and Ben Wyvis rising beyond it. And the Great Glen—there, where you can just see the patches of forest.'

His arm around her shoulders guided her head in the other direction to a vista of heather moorland, lit now by the light of the rising moon. And the old town, with its red sandstone buildings, and the river Ness running through it.

'You're right, Adam, it is breath-taking,' Meg agreed, but she wasn't sure whether it was the beauty of the moonlit

scene or Adam's nearness to her that was taking her breath
away.

She shivered.

'You're cold, Meg. We should get back,' Adam said,
concerned.

She assured him that she wasn't cold, but he opened the
door of the Land Rover and helped her to climb in. Meg,
sitting beside him as they drove back to the hotel, wasn't
sure whether she felt relieved or disappointed that she had
put a stop to that disturbing moment of nearness.

There was no one else around, other than the night porter, when they went into the hotel and up the wide staircase
to their rooms on the first floor.

Meg put her key in her door, and unlocked it.

'Goodnight, Adam,' she said softly. 'Thank you for
showing me what a beautiful place Inverness is.'

The big farmer made no reply to that. He looked down
at her, his eyes very dark. And then he said her name.

'Meg… Oh, Meg, lass.'

His kiss was gentle at first, gentle and warm. Then it was
not at all gentle, but urgent, demanding—a demand and an
urgency which there was no refusing.

Somehow they were in her room, with the door closed
behind them. Once he had said to her, 'This is not the time
or the place.' But here, in this dimly lit hotel room, was
the time and the place, and there was no turning back for
either of them.

Later—much later—with Adam's arms around her and
her head resting on the warm skin of his chest, she lay with
her eyes closed, wanting this moment, this closeness, to go
on for ever.

'Oh, Meg,' Adam said, his lips against her hair, 'I have
wanted to make love to you for so long. But I am thinking
it was not a very wise thing to do.'

She moved so that she could see his face.

'I wanted it as much as you did, Adam,' she told him, not quite steadily. 'You must know that. But why do you say it wasn't wise?'

He shook his head. 'For many reasons,' he said, his voice low. He leaned on his elbow and looked down at her and, with the moonlight filtering in through the curtains, she saw he was smiling. 'But I will not spoil the magic of this with regrets,' he told her. 'And magic it was. Now I had better get back to my own room for this is an old-fashioned hotel with none of your modern tea-making facilities. At eight o'clock a wee chambermaid will be bringing you a pot of tea, and perhaps it would be more discreet if she was to find you alone.'

He got out of bed and dressed. Meg lay in bed and looked at his lean, muscular body, her own still warm from their love-making.

'I'll see you at breakfast,' he murmured, and his lips brushed hers. 'What are you laughing at, woman?'

'I'm laughing at the thought of you maybe meeting someone, and your shoes and socks in your hands. I don't think that would be very discreet, Adam.'

When he had gone she lay in the darkness, wide-eyed with the wonder of what had just happened. She forced herself not to think of the way he'd said it hadn't been very wise, remembering, instead, that he wouldn't spoil the magic with regrets.

Oh, yes, Adam, Meg thought drowsily, oh, yes, it was magic.

As he had said, the little chambermaid brought her tea the next morning. Meg sat up in the bed she and Adam had shared, and drank her tea demurely and, she reminded herself, discreetly, smiling as she thought of Adam in his room next door, drinking his tea and also remembering last night.

Neither of them made any reference to it over breakfast

or on the way to the hospital, but as they walked towards the main entrance Adam stopped.

'Do you think it was heartless of me, Meg, not to be thinking of Jeannie last night?' he said, taking her by surprise. 'To be honest, there was no thought of anything but you and me when we were together.'

Meg shook her head.

'No, Adam,' she said very firmly. 'No, it wasn't heartless. You once said to me, "this is not the time or the place". Now I'm saying it to you—this is not the time or the place to be feeling guilty because just for a short time you forgot—we both forgot—to think about Jeannie, to be worried about her. I think perhaps you needed to think only of yourself just for once.'

He smiled.

'I wouldn't say only of myself,' he said softly. 'You came into the picture, too, Meg. And now I have made you blush.'

He touched her warm cheek lightly.

'Come along, let's see what Dr Robinson has to say.'

They knew, before the white-haired doctor said a word, that the news was good. He was smiling as he rose to meet them.

'We've done it, Mr Kerr—Meg,' he said. 'Jeannie is in remission, and her blood count is better than I expected. The white blood count has dropped, and I'm happy with the haemoglobin level. I want to keep her on a maintenance drug regime, and I don't expect any side-effects. We do still, of course, have to watch for infections. I'd like to see her in six months, but in the meantime take her home and let her lead as normal a life as she seems able to handle.'

He came with them to the children's ward, where Jeannie was already dressed and sitting on her bed, her cheeks flushed.

'Sister said I could get dressed,' she said. 'Dr Robinson, can I go to school tomorrow?'

The white-haired doctor laughed.

'Long may that enthusiasm continue, young lady,' he said. 'Yes, of course you can, Jeannie.' He went on, easily, 'Look, you may still get a bit tired sometimes, and I want you to be sensible about that and rest, even if you'd rather do what all the other children are doing, but by all means go to school tomorrow.'

'There's something special I want to do,' Jeannie said mysteriously. 'It's a secret.'

Next morning, when Meg dropped her off at school, she was still full of mysterious hints about her 'secret'.

'You'll know soon, Meg,' she promised.

With some misgivings, in spite of what Dr Robinson had said, Adam and Meg had agreed that Jeannie should go to school, but not for the whole day. Meg was to pick her up at lunchtime and take her home. Adam had phoned her teacher and told her that she could get hold of Meg at the surgery during the morning if she felt Jeannie should go home earlier.

That was all they'd talked about last night, Meg thought as she parked at the surgery. Accounts and book-keeping had to be done, Adam had said vaguely, and then he'd disappeared into his small office. Meg knew very well that there was no way there could be any repetition of the night before, here at Craigrannoch, but she had thought that perhaps they might have talked about it.

Anyway, she kept telling herself determinedly through the busy morning of surgery, the news about Jeannie was good, and it was good, too, to know that she herself was useful and helpful here in the surgery. It was a busy morning, with the changeable weather bringing glen folks with flu symptoms, chesty colds and various aches and pains.

'I think I'd welcome a straightforward broken leg,' Neil

said ruefully. 'Easier to deal with than some of these vague things. Are you coming tomorrow, Meg?'

'I hope so,' Meg said, taking her jacket from the peg. 'As long as Jeannie has coped with school today.'

'And the ceilidh?' Neil asked.

Meg hesitated, and then said carefully that perhaps she and Adam and Jeannie would be coming to it.

'Then I'll see you there,' Neil said. He smiled, but there was disappointment in his blue eyes.

Adam was in the kitchen, waiting for them, when they got back to the farm. Rex and Glen greeted Jeannie with enthusiasm. Glen was still moving stiffly, but at least he was able to walk.

Meg went up to her room to change out of her uniform, and when she came back down she paused at the kitchen door. Jeannie was sitting at the kitchen table, showing her father something, and the big farmer's dark head, bent over his small daughter, brought a rush of tenderness to Meg's heart.

'It's not quite finished, Daddy,' Jeannie said, 'but when it is I'll give it to Meg.'

The secret, Meg thought. I had better keep quiet.

'But it's a Mother's Day card, Jeannie,' Adam said.

'I know,' Jeannie replied, adding matter-of-factly, 'but I want to give it to Meg.'

Everything in Meg was still as she stood at the door, unseen, waiting for Adam to reply.

'I don't think that's a very good idea, Jeannie,' he said.

Meg saw nothing but dismay in his face.

Dismay which was echoed in her heart.

CHAPTER TEN

NEITHER Jeannie nor Adam had seen Meg.

'But why not, Daddy?' Jeannie said, bewildered. 'We made them at school. That was why I specially wanted to go today—because everyone had to finish their cards today. I hadn't even started, but Miss Hamilton let me stay in at playtime so that I could finish my card for Meg. Look, I drew Glen on it 'cos I knew she would like that.'

Silently, Meg turned and went back upstairs. She didn't want to hear Adam's reply, and she didn't need to because of that look of dismay she had seen on his face. Dismay because Jeannie had made a Mother's Day card for her.

She sat on her bed. The girl in the mirror looked back at her, all colour drained from her face. Only now could she admit to herself that she'd hoped...she'd dreamed... Now the hopes and the dreams were gone. Painfully, she faced the truth. Adam's kisses, the night they had spent in each other's arms—none of that had meant to him what it had meant to her. He'd been lonely, and she'd been there. That was all. She'd read too much into what had happened.

He had, she reminded herself, said to her, 'I am thinking it was not a very wise thing to do.' He had been, of course, so right in that. He would think it had been even more unwise if he'd known how much she'd built on that night.

She lifted her chin, and held her head high. He doesn't know, and he won't know, she told herself. The girl in the mirror looked back at her, defiant now.

When she went downstairs for the second time Adam was sitting in his chair, reading the paper, and Jeannie was watching TV. She hadn't been crying—she wasn't a child who cried easily—but her grey eyes were suspiciously bright. When Glen rose from his place near the stove and hobbled over to greet Meg, Jeannie rose from the couch, knelt beside him and put her arms around him.

'I'm sure he remembers when you went to the cave and took him food, Meg,' she said, her voice muffled against the dog's silky coat. 'You'll always be special to him because of that.'

It was all Meg could do not to hold the little girl close and tell her—

Tell her what? Meg asked herself. That Jeannie herself had become special to Meg, and that she always would be? No, there was no way she could say anything like that now that she knew how Adam felt.

She asked Jeannie about Colin, and said how glad he would be to see how much better Glen was now. Then, hoping that her voice was steady, she asked Adam if there was any news from the other farmers of the sheep-killer dog.

'None at all,' Adam replied, putting down his newspaper. 'Will Mackay over at the far side of the glen lost a sheep two nights ago, apparently, but no one saw anything of the dog.' He smiled. 'But everyone knows now that our Glen is innocent.'

Our Glen.

Yours and Jeannie's, Meg thought, not mine, Adam, because that isn't what you want.

'Well, Jeannie,' she said brightly, 'no problem about me going to work again tomorrow since you seem to be set for school.' She turned to Adam. 'Is that all right with you, Adam?'

The big man's dark eyes rested on her face, questioning.

'Of course,' he replied after a moment. 'I'm sure the two doctors and Beth Drummond will be glad of your help. You must be glad to be back at the surgery, I'm sure.'

'Yes, I am,' Meg agreed.

That was true. Already the routine of morning surgery and then going out on house visits had a reassuring familiarity, and she was beginning to know some of the patients.

'Mrs Barr? Morag Barr?' she asked, getting a card ready. Then, realising who her patient was, she said, 'Oh, Mrs Barr, you were here for your flu injection a couple of weeks ago, weren't you? I met your husband at Craigrannoch.'

Mrs Barr nodded. 'Robert was right glad it wasn't the wee lassie's dog at the sheep,' she said. 'Not that it helps us, mind, for it means our sheep are still at risk.'

The surgery door opened, and Dr Macrae's white head appeared.

'Oh, Morag, it's yourself,' he said as Meg handed him the card. 'Come along through.'

With considerable difficulty, Mrs Barr stood up.

'I don't need to tell you, Dr Macrae, it's my back again,' she said, and she tried to smile. 'All I did was bend to put the milk back in the fridge, but I must have done it awkwardly. And I did what you told me last time—the bag of peas from the deep-freeze on my back. It helped a bit, but not enough.'

She was the last patient, and at the old doctor's nod Meg followed them through to the surgery. Gently, Dr Macrae moved his patient's legs, first one, then the other, testing the mobility and establishing the point of strain.

'Well, I'm going to give you an anti-inflammatory injection, Morag, and a prescription as well, and I think you'll get away with it this time. But, sooner or later, you're going to have to have something done about that disc.'

A little later, when Meg helped Mrs Barr to stand up, he handed her the prescription.

'Remember, now, two days' bed rest and then up, but move slowly and carefully. Let me know how you're doing when you've been up and about for a couple of days.'

The farmer's wife put the prescription in her handbag.

'It's just that we're coming to the busiest time on the farm, Dr Macrae, and I don't think they'd manage if I was to be away in the hospital,' she said apologetically. 'And, from what you say, I'd be out of action for some time.'

Dr Macrae opened the door for her.

'Aye, that you would,' he agreed, 'but you'd be well advised to make it a priority, otherwise you'll have no choice about it at all.'

When she'd gone he shook his head.

'It will be a laminectomy or a diskectomy,' he said, 'and that disc will not be choosing the most convenient time to rupture. I'm going to have a word with Robert Barr, I think. Oh, Meg, here is the list Beth left for you. I see Andrew Ritchie should have been here today—maybe you could look in and see how he is. He's a great one for conveniently forgetting to keep his appointment, especially when he knows I've seen him in and out of the pub at the hotel.'

He was the old man with the ulcer, Meg remembered as she got into her car. Maybe she should look in on him before she went on to do the two bed-baths.

There was no reply when she rang the doorbell of the cottage near the school.

'Mr Ritchie?' she called, and she knocked on the window. Then, a little hesitantly, she tried the handle of the door and found it unlocked.

As she went into the small living-room she saw that the fire had gone out. A half-open door presumably led to the bedroom. Suddenly decisive, she went through, her breath catching in her throat as she saw the old man in the bed.

He was barely conscious, and he had lost a great deal of blood. He was obviously in considerable pain.

'Mr Ritchie, I'm going to call the doctor,' Meg said firmly, not sure whether the old man could hear her.

She had seen the phone in the small entrance hall, and

when Neil replied she told him quickly and concisely about Andrew Ritchie's condition.

'I'll be right there,' he said. Five minutes later she heard his car draw up, and hurried to meet him.

'How is he?' he asked, at the door.

'He's in shock,' Meg told him, 'and he's lost a lot of blood. I've cleaned him up as well as I can, but I didn't want to move him any more than I had to. He's in considerable pain.'

She stood back while the young doctor examined the man on the bed.

'The ulcer has perforated, of course,' he said, his voice low. 'He needs to be operated on. I'll phone for an ambulance, and then we'll give him some blood and do what we can to stabilise him.'

As soon as he'd made the phone call he gave the old man an injection to sedate him, then he and Meg set up a drip. Old Andrew had lost so much blood that his pulse was thready and his blood pressure dangerously low.

'But it isn't going any lower—we're holding him,' Neil said wearily an hour later. 'I hope the ambulance comes soon.'

Ten minutes later it arrived. Carefully, the ambulance men eased the unconscious man, now grey-faced and groaning softly, onto a stretcher.

'What do you think of his chances, Neil?' Meg asked, as the ambulance drove off.

'He's not very great,' Neil said soberly, 'but, thanks to even the small amount of blood we managed to get into him, he has a chance. If they can just hold him until they get him into the theatre he might make it.'

He looked down at her.

'And maybe he'll learn to treat that ulcer with more respect.'

He put one arm around her shoulders.

'You did a great job, Meg,' he said. 'Thanks for help.'

There was barely time for Meg to finish her list of vis, but she managed her two bed-baths, the diabetes injectio and a check on the old lady with bronchitis before it wa time to pick Jeannie up from school.

Colin was with her, a wide grin on his freckled face.

'I'm coming to see Glen,' he told her. 'Jeannie says he can walk now. And he must be feeling grand, and him with his name cleared.'

Gravely, Meg agreed that it certainly must make Glen feel good. There was no doubt that the collie was pleased to see both children, his plumed tail wagging in greeting as he rose from his favourite sunny corner in the yard when they got out of the car.

'And what are you doing here, Colin Cameron? Have you not a home to go to?' Betsy demanded, but Meg knew by now—and she could see that Colin and Jeannie did, too—that the old housekeeper was pleased to see the small boy. 'And I suppose you'll be hoping for something to eat?'

Colin's red head nodded emphatically.

'I was telling my mum about the grand soup you make, Auntie Betsy,' he said, his dark eyes limpid. 'Maybe you could write down the recipe for her.'

Betsy sniffed, not managing to hide her pleasure.

'Aye, well, there's nothing to beat good home-made soup,' she agreed, 'but as for a recipe it's just whatever there is handy. Come in, then, and have a plate of soup.'

Meg was glad the boy had come home with Jeannie and happy to see the little girl brighter than she'd been when Meg had dropped her at school that morning. She thought that Adam, too, was relieved to have Colin there for he could talk to the children rather than to her.

'You'll all be coming to the ceilidh on Saturday, Mr

Kerr?' Colin asked, accepting another piece of Betsy's crunchy biscuit,

'I'm not sure, Colin,' Adam began, but Jeannie's outraged gasp stopped him.

'Not go to the ceilidh?' she said. 'Daddy, we can't miss it. Everyone will be there. And Meg has never been to a ceilidh.'

For a moment Adam's dark eyes met Meg's, then he looked away.

'I don't know that a ceilidh here in the glen is much in Meg's line, Jeannie,' he said, so dismissively that for some perverse reason Meg's instinctive rejoinder that she would love to go to the ceilidh was never uttered.

Instead, she smiled and shrugged and said he was probably right, but if Jeannie wanted to go she didn't mind.

'We have to go, Daddy,' Jeannie said imperiously. She turned to Meg. 'Remember, Meg, last time Dr Patterson was here he said we must come to the ceilidh. And he said he would dance ''The Dashing White Sergeant'' with us— that's the one that you either need a man with two ladies or a lady with two men.'

Adam stood up.

'In that case, of course we'll go,' he said. 'I'm going back to the field now—I've a ewe who might need a hand with her birthing.' He bent and patted Glen's head. 'Not you, boy, not yet—maybe next week. Come, Rex.'

With the younger collie at his heels, he strode out. Through the kitchen window Meg could see his tall figure, his dark head held high, as he hurried away.

'What will you wear on Saturday, Meg?' Jeannie asked.

'I don't know,' Meg replied, and she couldn't help thinking how differently she might have felt about this ceilidh if she hadn't seen that moment of complete dismay on Adam's face because Jeannie had made a Mother's Day card for her.

All the same, when it came to Saturday she found herself looking at her wardrobe and wondering if it would be too cold to wear her silky turquoise dress. She held it up against her and looked in the mirror, her brown curls tilted as she remembered wearing it for her engagement party. Simon, his ring on her left hand, the plans they had made—all that belonged to another life, she realised with some surprise, a life that somehow didn't seem real now. Even the big bustling hospital had lost its reality.

However, the hospital, or another like it, was something she would have to think about some time soon, she knew. If Jeannie's remission continued there was no need for her here. In any case, it would perhaps be the best thing for her to move on.

The best thing, the most sensible thing. But there was an ache in her heart at the thought of leaving Jeannie and Glen. She stopped there, unwilling—or unable—to take the thought any further.

'Darn it, I'll wear the dress,' she said aloud, and she slipped the silky folds over her head. Yes, she thought, yes, as she brushed her brown curls back from her face and found the eye-shadow that matched the dress perfectly.

Jeannie had already gone downstairs, and Meg had heard Adam close the door of his room a little while ago. She went downstairs, all at once self-conscious.

'Meg, you look like a princess,' Jeannie said, her eyes wide. 'Doesn't she, Daddy?'

Adam's eyes were very dark, his face still.

'That she does,' he said, his voice low. 'You look real bonny, Meg.'

You look pretty good yourself, Adam, Meg thought. She had never seen him wearing a kilt before, and his tall, strong figure seemed so right for the swing of the tartan, his broad shoulders made for the tweed jacket.

'I like your tartan pinafore dress, Jeannie,' she said quickly.

'And my frilly blouse,' Jeannie pointed out. 'They didn't fit me when I was fat because of the pills, but they're all right now.'

The old housekeeper came through from her own room.

'A bonny dress, Meg,' she said, adding practically, 'but you'll no' be warm enough—the school hall is a draughty place. Wait a minute.'

She bustled out, and came back a few minutes later with a white mohair stole.

'Colin's folks gave it to me,' she said, 'but a warm cardigan does a better job for me. Here, you'll likely be glad of it later, Meg.'

The school hall had been decorated with streamers and balloons, and as they walked across the playground they could hear the sound of foot-tapping and very Scottish music.

'That will be Sandy the fiddler and his band,' Betsy said with satisfaction. 'He's wearing on, is Sandy, but he has a grand touch with the fiddle.'

Sandy the fiddler didn't look any older than Betsy herself, Meg thought, but she wouldn't have dared to say that.

The transformed school hall was filled with people—old people, young people, children, babies. There were smiles and nods to Meg from people she had met in the surgery or around the village, and Colin and a dark-haired little girl came running up to claim Jeannie and take her to a corner near the stage, where most of the children had gathered. Meg went with Betsy to add two more laden plates of food to the already groaning tables, and as she made her way around the dancers she found Neil Patterson at her side, wearing a kilt, as so many of the men were, and looking very handsome in it.

'Don't get in the way of this lot,' he said, and she could

barely hear him above the sound of the music. 'They're doing an eightsome reel, and they're giving it stick.'

'They're certainly enjoying themselves,' Meg agreed, as the dancers whirled and turned, their arms joined. A fearsome yell went out from a big burly farmer as he whirled his partner off her feet, and in spite of the background noise Meg jumped.

'Och, they're only hooching,' Neil said, smiling. He turned as Adam joined them. 'Adam, I'm just after telling Meg that this is just hooching—it isn't a war cry.' And then, a little challengingly, he said, 'Were you coming to look for her, then?'

Adam smiled, but his dark eyes were distant.

'No,' he said, 'I was on my way to have a word with Robert Barr, but I see Ailie Fraser is to be singing so we'd better sit down.'

Miraculously, it seemed to Meg, the hall cleared and everyone sat down, the children cross-legged on the floor and babies being handed from one set of willing arms to another. Meg had met Ailie Fraser in the surgery when she'd brought her teenage daughter in with laryngitis. Dark-haired, dark-eyed and a little plump, she stood up in front of the stage with her hands clasped and began to sing, unaccompanied. Her voice was low and sweet as she sang in Gaelic, and although Meg couldn't understand the words there was something so haunting, so sad, that she felt her eyes fill with tears.

There was silence in the hall when she'd finished—even the children sitting wide-eyed. Then, with a smile, the young woman held out her hand to the old fiddler, he began to play again and the spell was broken.

'That was so beautiful. What was she singing about, Adam?' Meg asked.

'"The Flowers of the Forest",' Adam told her.

'About a long-ago battle, and the men who were lost in it, and the women who will always mourn them.'

He stood up.

'We'd better have something to eat,' he said. 'I see the teacups are out now beside the food.'

'And the whisky glasses,' Neil said, standing up, too. 'Meg, just after you left today there was a message from Inverness. Andrew Ritchie is doing fine. He'll be home in a few days.'

The three of them had just reached the laden tables when Beth touched Neil's arm.

'You promised to dance the "Gay Gordons" with me, Neil,' she said. 'Come on.'

The young doctor went off, shaking his head and muttering that it was a terrible name for a man like him to be associated with.

Gavin Ferguson and his wife greeted Adam, and Meg took her plate of food and went to sit with John Drummond for a while. From where she was sitting she could see Jeannie and Colin and the other children in their class, eating hot dogs and drinking lemonade. Jeannie's cheeks were flushed and her eyes were bright. I'll watch her, Meg thought, and just make sure she doesn't overtire herself.

'She's having a grand time, is she not?' John said, also looking at Jeannie. He looked around. 'Adam, I was just saying to Meg your wee Jeannie is fair enjoying this.'

'She certainly is,' Adam agreed. 'She's all right, isn't she, Meg?'

'Yes, she is,' Meg assured him. 'A few hours of this won't do her any harm.'

The big farmer's dark eyes were on his small daughter.

'She looks just like any of the other children, does she not?' he said, his voice low. For the first time he's daring to let himself hope, Meg thought, and in spite of the distance she'd felt between them she put her hand on his arm.

'Adam,' she began, not sure what she was going to say.

At almost the same moment someone else said his name.

Helen, her blonde hair sleek and smooth, her black sheath clinging to her slim body, held out both hands to him. A little awkwardly, Adam took them in his.

'You are a very wicked man, Adam Kerr,' Helen said gaily. 'I hear you were in Inverness, and you didn't even call me.'

'It was only for one night, Helen,' Adam said. For one startled moment Meg found his eyes meeting hers in a shared memory of that one night. 'I'm afraid I didn't have time.'

Meg wasn't sure if she imagined that Helen's eyes flickered to her briefly, but the next moment the blonde girl shrugged.

'I was probably busy anyway,' she said. She raised one slim brown arm and waved across the room. 'I just came over to say hello—I'm with the Frasers, and Nick and Rob Hamilton. We looked in to keep my folks happy—now we're off to the dinner-dance at the Spindrift hotel. Much more my scene. See you some time, Adam.'

It was so blatant that she was writing Adam off. Meg looked at him, distressed for him.

'Yes, I'm sure that will be more Helen's scene,' Adam murmured, and his faint smile told Meg that he wasn't in the slightest bit bothered. Ridiculously, her heart lifted.

Jeannie came running across the hall to them, her hand in Neil Patterson's.

'Remember, Meg, we're going to dance "The Dashing White Sergeant" with Dr Patterson,' she said breathlessly. 'Isn't this a lovely ceilidh? Daddy, will you watch me dancing?'

Adam assured her that he would, and sat beside John as the young doctor took Meg's hand and the three of them joined the waiting dancers.

It was completely confusing for Meg, turning and whirling between Neil and Jeannie, but there were friendly hands to guide her in the right direction, and friendly laughter when that didn't work and she found herself, breathless and bewildered, looking around for her partners.

'You did that very well, Meg,' Jeannie told her, when the music ended and the dancers moved off the floor. 'Didn't she, Daddy?'

'Yes, she did,' Adam agreed. He looked at Meg. 'Maybe we had better be going home soon?'

'I'm not tired,' Jeannie said indignantly. 'Colin's mum says he can stay right till the end.' She looked up at Neil, her wide grey eyes appealing. 'Don't you think this is doing me a lot of good, Dr Patterson?'

Neil laughed. 'I'm not going to argue with your dad, Jeannie, but perhaps just a wee while longer.' He looked down at Meg. 'And just to show you a different kind of Scottish dancing, come now and dance "Waltz Country" with me.'

There were slow and sweet waltz tunes, familiar even to Meg, and a courtly foursome, dancing together and then breaking again into couples. Neil's arms held her as close as possible when they were dancing on their own.

'I always thought I liked the boisterous dances best, but tonight I prefer this kind,' Neil murmured, and she could feel his breath against her hair. 'We dance well together, Meg.'

Meg tried to move back a little, but his arms held her firmly. Across the room Adam stood, watching them, his lean brown face very still and his eyes very dark.

He doesn't like me dancing like this with Neil, Meg realised, taken aback. Why should that bother him? she thought, remembering the dismay on his face because

Jeannie wanted to give her a Mother's Day card?

Adam Kerr, she thought, disturbed, I will never understand you!

CHAPTER ELEVEN

JEANNIE fell asleep in Meg's arms five minutes after they left the school hall. Betsy was staying on to help to clear up when the ceilidh finally finished—and that wouldn't be for some time, Meg thought, judging by the noise and the enjoyment level—and she would spend the night with her sister.

So there were just the three of them, driving back to the farm. Adam was driving and Meg was beside him with the sleeping child in her arms. Almost like a family, Meg thought with sadness. Except that Adam doesn't want us to be a family.

The two dogs, curled up beside the warmth of the big stove, greeted them with enthusiasm, but all it needed was a quick and barely audible command from Adam and Rex and Glen lay down with their noses on their paws, and their ears alert, while Adam carried Jeannie upstairs to her room.

She stirred slightly as Meg put her pyjamas on her.

'I'm not tired, you know,' she murmured. 'I could easily have stayed much longer at the ceilidh.'

'I'm sure you could,' Meg agreed, buttoning Jeannie's pyjama top, 'but I was tired, and I think your Daddy was, too. Here he is with your hot-water bottle.'

Adam slipped the hot-water bottle in at Jeannie's feet, and Meg tucked her in. She bent and kissed the little girl's soft cheek.

'Goodnight, Jeannie,' she said softly, and all at once her heart was almost too full for words.

'Night, Meg. Night, Daddy,' Jeannie murmured. Meg, looking back as she half closed the door, saw that Jeannie was almost asleep again. She saw, too, that Adam was looking at her, unsmiling—unsmiling, and sad, she thought, bewildered.

'It's late,' she said, more abruptly than she'd meant to. 'Thank you for taking me to the ceilidh, Adam, it was quite an experience.'

'Yes, it would certainly be different from anything you've ever done before,' Adam replied. Without a pause he went on, 'Young Neil was telling me that he is trying to persuade you to join him in Libya with his Médecins Sans Frontières. That would be an exciting life for you, Meg—more exciting than the glen.'

'It's incredibly demanding, working in these Third World countries,' Meg said quickly, 'but, yes, it would certainly be exciting.' Then some perverse impulse made her go on before she could lose her courage. 'I do need to think about what I'm going to do, Adam. With Jeannie so much better, I don't think you really need me here for her.'

In the dim light of the landing he looked down at her. She knew very well that he was thinking the same thing she was. Yes, Jeannie was better—but for how long? I can't stay here much longer, Meg thought. I can't allow myself to become even more emotionally involved with Jeannie. And with Adam. For Jeannie's sake, as much as for my own, the break has to be made.

'Yes,' Adam said very quietly, 'I was wondering when you would be thinking that way. There is no need to be rushing into leaving, Meg, but perhaps you are right. Will you let me know when you come to any decision?'

Meg turned away.

'Yes, I'll do that,' she said. She went into her room and closed the door, all at once not even able to say goodnight to Adam. She sat on her bed, and she could no longer hold back the tears. Slow, silent tears ran down her cheeks, tears for the end of the dreams she'd had.

That night in Inverness, with Adam's arms around her, his lips and his body demanding and urgent. Her own passionate response to that demand. Falling asleep in each other's arms and waking, still in each other's arms. Would she ever be able to forget that? How could it be that it had meant so much to her and so little to Adam?

It was a long time before she fell asleep, and when she woke next morning she found her cheeks still wet with tears. But her mind was made up. It would be better for all of them if she went away as soon as possible. Somehow she would have to find the courage to tell Jeannie.

Perhaps, she thought, when Betsy's nephew brought her back to the farm, she should have a word with the old housekeeper in fairness, and tell her what she was meaning to do.

Colin had come with his father, and as it was Sunday, he and Jeannie went off with Adam to see some new-born lambs.

'Away you go, Keith. We'll see that Colin gets back later,' Betsy told her nephew when he left. 'You've got all these chairs to sort out at the school, remember.'

Meg took the old lady's arm and sat her down.

'I have to do your blood-pressure check-up, Betsy,' she said, 'so just calm down. Remember what I told you my nursing textbook says—"The patient should be encouraged to adopt a more tranquil attitude to life."'

Unwillingly, Betsy smiled.

'Aye, that sounds fine, but I don't think I'm likely to become very tranquil at this stage of my life, lass.'

Meg adjusted the baunomometer, and pumped it up.

'A big improvement, Betsy,' she said. 'The diastolic reading is below eighty now, and I know Dr Macrae will be very pleased.'

'Such wee white pills to be making a difference,' Betsy said. 'And there's no doubt I don't have that headache in the mornings now. I'm real glad you persuaded me to go to the doctor, Meg.'

She went over to the kitchen sink, and began to peel potatoes. 'And what did you think of Lady Muck's outfit?' she asked. Although her back was to Meg, there was no mistaking the fact that she was smiling.

'Lady Muck?' Meg asked.

Betsy turned.

'Helen Ferguson in her ''little black dress'',' she said. 'And her behaving as if she was doing us all a favour, just by looking in for five minutes.'

'I thought she looked very smart,' Meg said truthfully. Then, unable to stop herself, she said, 'But, Betsy, I thought Helen was one of your favourite people.'

Betsy coloured. 'Aye well, I was wrong about her,' she said hurriedly. 'She seemed so interested in Jeannie, always asking about her, always coming here to see her. I just wanted my wee lassie to have a mother, Meg, and I thought, with Helen belonging to the glen, that would be a good thing—for Jeannie and for Adam. But I see now she would just be wanting Adam to live her kind of life, and there would be no happiness for him. Or, likely, for her. Certainly, she wouldn't be the right mother for Jeannie.'

Meg barely heard the last of what Betsy was saying. She went over to the old woman.

'What do you mean—that it would be a good thing, Helen belonging to the glen?' she asked slowly.

Betsy put the last of the potatoes in the pot and set it on the big stove.

'Maybe I'm speaking out of turn,' she said, her voice low, 'but you'll not know about Jeannie's mother. Och, she was a nice enough lassie was Shelagh, but she came from Edinburgh and she never fitted in here in the glen. It was all right at first. She was always laughing and singing, and she seemed right happy, but she wearied of the quiet life here in the glen and she was always finding a reason to go to the city. She missed the bright lights, Adam said. He was always making excuses for her, and he was never anything but loyal, but I ken fine that by the time Jeannie was a year old Adam knew very well that she wasn't happy here in the glen.'

She moved the pot of potatoes as the water began to bubble.

'And then there was the accident,' she said quietly. 'She was on her way to have a few days with her friends in Edinburgh when it happened. It's just a mercy that she always left Jeannie here with me.'

What was it Adam had said when he'd spoken of his wife? Something about when they were first married she'd been so bright, always laughing, but that she had changed and the brightness and the laughter had gone.

What Betsy had said made Meg forget that she had intended to tell the old housekeeper that she would soon be going away. Through the rest of that day she couldn't put out of her mind the thought of Adam and his young wife, so happy at first, so bright. Then, slowly, Adam would have seen that the glen had been too quiet for her, that she'd wanted to get out of it—away from the farm.

Away from him?

Certainly, he would have thought that more and more. Already, because she had come to know him, Meg understood that he would have blamed himself for not seeing that this was not the right life for a girl like Shelagh. A girl who didn't belong to the glen.

After she'd died he would have been determined that he wouldn't make the same mistake again. He would think of Shelagh, and he would think of the silkies.

What was it he'd said, that day beside the sea, when he'd told her the story of the silkies? 'And all he will have is the sound of her singing, and the memory of her, for all the rest of his life.'

Meg remembered, too, what she had said.   'It's a lovely story, Adam, but so sad.'

'Yes,' he had said, 'it is a sad story. But surely a man should have more sense than to keep a seal-woman away from the sea, to keep her in a place that is not meant for her?'

That day she'd told herself it was only a story, but she could see now so clearly that Adam had been thinking of Shelagh. And thinking that he wouldn't again make the same mistake, that he wouldn't again try to keep a seal-woman in a place that was not meant for her.

That was why he'd said so many strange and disturbing things. A kiss, which he'd said they should both forget. A night spent in each other's arms, a night which he felt had not been wise. And what he'd said to Jeannie about the card she wanted to give Meg for Mother's Day—'I don't think that is a good idea.'

Of course he'd say that, Meg thought that night as she sat on the window-seat, looking out at the moonlit farm-yard. He wouldn't want to risk loving me, letting Jeannie love me and then having to see that I was unhappy here in the glen and that I wanted to go away.

Even now that she understood, her heart was heavy. Knowing how Adam felt didn't mean that she would be able to change it. What could she do, anyway? Go to him and tell him that he was wrong about her—that she loved him, she loved Jeannie and she wouldn't want to leave them or the farm and the glen?

He would look at her, his eyes dark, his face unsmiling, and he would say politely that it was all very well, but he had seen how Shelagh had changed.

I can't just give up, Meg thought.

She put on her dressing-gown and went out of her room

and across the landing. Adam's door was closed. He would be asleep with one arm flung out, the way she'd seen him asleep that night in Inverness. He would come to the door, she would say what she wanted to say, and he would...he would...

Meg's hand, ready to knock, dropped. She couldn't bear to see the dismissal and the rejection on his face. She could be wrong in all that she had been thinking, she told herself. Perhaps her earlier thoughts had been right and that it was much more simple than that—a lonely man, a young woman there, ready to fall into his arms. And, boy, did I do that, Meg thought bitterly.

She turned away and went back to her room.

The telephone rang while they were having breakfast the next morning, and Adam went to answer it.

When he came back he bent and patted Glen's head.

'Well, boy, that's the end of the sheep-killing story,' he said. He sat at the table. 'That was Bob Ferguson—he stayed out last night because he'd found a sheep attacked the night before. No, Jeannie, the sheep was all right— something had scared the dog off. Anyway, Bob decided he would just sit in the shepherd's hut and wait. Sure enough, about midnight the dog came. He saw him in the moonlight as clear as anything—a big Alsatian—and he shot him just as the dog went for one of the new lambs.'

Jeannie burst into tears.

'The poor dog,' she sobbed.

Meg took the little girl in her arms, and held her close.

'Think of all the poor sheep, Jeannie,' Adam said help- lessly. 'And this was a lamb he was after.'

Jeannie's sobs were even more heartfelt.

'I know, but—but I keep thinking if Glen had been found near the sheep he would have been killed. And—and some- one must have loved the Alsatian.'

There were no words to comfort her so Meg held her close and let her cry. Above Jeannie's fair head Adam's eyes met hers and he shook his head, at a loss.

'Better, Jeannie?' Meg said after a while, and Jeannie nodded. Meg dried her face and brushed the thick, fair hair back from her forehead.

'Give Glen a good cuddle,' she suggested. 'And Rex. That will help.'

And it did. Jeannie hugged first Glen and then Rex, and in a little while she went out into the farmyard, one collie on each side of her.

'I didn't know what to do with her,' Adam admitted.

'She just had to have a cry and get it out of her system,' Meg said. 'She's a tender-hearted little girl, Adam, and the thought of the dog being shot was too much for her. Where had he come from, anyway?'

'From the next glen,' Adam told her. 'He wasn't a farm dog. He belonged to someone in the village.'

To her horror, Meg felt her own eyes fill with tears. Jeannie was right—someone must have loved him.

A little awkwardly, Adam smiled.

'I'm not going to have you crying, too, am I?' he asked.

Meg brushed the back of her hand across her eyes.

'No, I'm all right,' she said. All at once, in the warm familiarity of the big farm kitchen, with Adam close to her and smiling, she almost found the courage to risk her pride and say the things she wanted to say. But a curtain seemed to come over the big farmer's face and he drew back so she was glad that she'd said nothing.

Without any more discussion between Adam and herself, the school days had fallen into a pattern. Meg took Jeannie to school, spent the morning either helping in the surgery or doing some of the house calls for the district nurse, then collected Jeannie when school finished.

On the day after the news about the dog Meg hurried

away from her exercise session with John, arriving at
school just as the bell rang. Rather to her surprise, Jeannie
came across the playground on her own, walking slowly.

She looked all right, Meg thought, trying to still her instinctive concern. There were no shadows under her eyes
and she wasn't any paler than usual. But she was quiet.

'Hi,' she said to the little girl. 'I was almost late, wasn't
I?' She looked around. 'Colin not out?'

At that moment he came running across the playground.
He handed Jeannie a white envelope.

'You forgot to take your card, Jeannie,' he said breathlessly. 'Miss Hamilton said to bring it to you. I wish it was
Sunday so that I could give mine to my mum.'

Jeannie's cheeks were now a fiery red as she snatched
the card from Colin.

'I didn't need it anyway,' she said, quite rudely. She
turned to Meg. 'Can we go now, Meg?'

'Aren't you coming to the farm today, Colin?' Meg
asked, but Colin told her he had soccer practice.

Jeannie was quiet on the way home, and it seemed better
to let her be, Meg thought, concerned.

She had forgotten that this Sunday was Mother's Day,
and she made a mental note to send flowers to her mother
and phone. But that didn't help the silent little girl, sitting
beside her.

On the drive back to the farm Meg knew that she had to
do something. For Jeannie and for herself. She couldn't
walk out of the little girl's life, without looking back. It
wasn't just Adam and herself—it was Adam and Jeannie,
and herself and Jeannie. We belong together, Meg thought
with growing conviction, the three of us, and I have to
make Adam see that. I have to risk being hurt, rejected. I
love Adam, and I love Jeannie.

The rain, which had been threatening all day, started as
Meg drew up at the back door of the farmhouse. Heavy

black clouds and a rising wind promised a storm, and already the low foothills beyond the farm were hidden behind driving sheets of rain. Meg was undeterred.

She organised Jeannie with her homework at the big kitchen table, with Glen moving from the stove to lie at her feet.

'Betsy,' she said, 'I'm going out.'

'Out?' the old housekeeper repeated. 'In this? Dinna be daft, lassie.'

Meg zipped up her anorak and pulled her boots on.

'Where's Adam?' she asked, and added when she saw Betsy's questioning eyes, 'I have to talk to him about something.'

Betsy shook her head in despair.

'He's in the field beside the loch,' she said, 'but surely it can wait, Meg.'

No, it can't, Meg thought, because I might lose my courage.

There was the deep rumble of nearby thunder, and then lightning streaked across the sky. Meg was soaked before she was halfway along the path beside the loch, and she realised that she would be lucky to find Adam in this, because she would barely be able to see more than halfway across the field.

She opened the gate, closing it behind her, and peered into the driving rain. Then she heard a short, sharp bark. Rex. She pulled her hood closer around her head and made for the sound.

'Adam!' she called, without much hope of him hearing her. 'Adam!'

Then, unbelievably, he was beside her.

'What in the world are you doing out in this, Meg?' he shouted above the rumbling thunder. 'Is something wrong?'

She shook her head.

'No, there's nothing wrong.' Then she said, 'Yes, there is.'

Now that she was here she didn't know what to say. All she knew was that she had to do something, to make this dear, stubborn man see sense.

She stood on tiptoe, and kissed him.

Their faces were wet with rain, and Adam's lips were cold against hers. He stood stiffly, resisting, for a long time, and then, slowly, she felt that resistance crumble. He put his arms around her, and held her close to him.

His kiss was so urgent, so searching, so demanding, that she was hardly conscious of him half lifting her, half carrying her, to the comparative shelter of the shepherd's hut on the shore of the loch.

'Now,' Adam said, not quite steadily, 'will you tell me what this is all about, Meg?'

Meg took a deep breath.

'Adam, I love you,' she said, and her own voice was steady. 'I love you, and I love Jeannie, and I will not be like the seal-woman and go away and leave you nothing but memories. I want to stay with you and Jeannie for the rest of my life.'

He looked down at her, his dark eyes searching her face as if, she thought, he longed to believe her but he hardly dared to.

'I mean it, Adam,' she said quietly. 'I mean it with all my heart.'

Meg wondered afterwards when it was that the storm had ended.

For there was nothing else in the world but the two of them, sitting on a broken bench in the rough hut, Adam's arms holding her as if he would never let her go.

At last, when they managed to draw apart, his lips leaving hers reluctantly, there was a time for words, for explanations.

'Why did you stop Jeannie from giving me the card for Mother's Day, Adam?' Meg asked, and she told him of the day she'd overheard Jeannie, talking about the card. And of how she'd felt when she'd seen the dismay on his face.

'I thought you didn't want me—on a permanent basis,' she said, a little shakily. 'I remembered other things you'd said, and I thought you were completely thrown at the thought of anything other than a…' No, she couldn't use the words, 'one-night stand'. Not now, not when Adam was looking at her the way he was.

'Meg, Meg, lass,' he said, so tenderly that her breath caught in her throat. 'It wasn't that at all. I was so afraid that if Jeannie gave you a card for Mother's Day, and you as fond of her as I knew you were, you would feel that you couldn't hurt her and that you would feel tied to her. And to me.'

'Emotional blackmail,' Meg said wonderingly. 'How could we both be so wrong about each other?'

Adam's arms tightened around her.

'And when I saw you dancing with Neil Patterson at the ceilidh,' he said, 'I was even more certain that a young fellow like him could give you a life that would be more right for you. You looked so right together, the two of you.'

'I like Neil, of course I do,' Meg said after a moment, 'but that's all.' Then, touching his lips with one hand, she said, not quite steadily, 'Adam, how could you have any doubts about the way I felt about you after that night in Inverness?'

Adam smiled, and now the shadows had gone from his dark eyes.

'I knew how you felt then,' he said quietly, 'but I thought you might have regrets later, that you might grow weary of living in the glen.'

Meg hesitated, but only for a moment.

'Like Shelagh did?' she asked him.

He didn't seem surprised that she knew.

'Yes,' he said. 'Like Shelagh. It was a terrible thing, Meg, to see the joy and the laughter leave her, to see her quiet and longing always to get away from the glen. A longing that made her forget, I think, that we loved each other. She was like a bird imprisoned in a cage the last year.'

'Or like one of your silkies?' Meg said. She took both his hands in hers. 'Adam, I will say it again—I will not be like that. I want to be here with you and with Jeannie, and I promise you that will not change.'

His eyes held hers for an apparent eternity. Then he nodded.

'Yes, my own Meg, I can see that is a promise you will not break.' Not quite steadily, his lips once again seeking hers, he said, 'Oh, Meg, Meg, *mo chridhe.*'

It was a long time before she asked him what it was that he'd said.

'You said it once before,' she reminded him, 'and you said then you would tell me some time what the words meant. Say it again, Adam, and tell me.'

'Mo chridhe,' he murmured, his lips against her cheek. 'It means many things, Meg, lass. Heart's delight, heart of my heart. Will that do to start with?'

'It will do very well,' Meg replied, her own voice less than steady.

Adam stood up, drawing her to her feet with him.

'I think we should be getting back home,' he said. 'The storm is over, and the sheep are none the worse for Rex has herded them all to the sheltered corner in the lee of the hill. Look, is he not a tactful lad, lying there with his back to us? Right, boy, home now.'

The black and white collie, lying at the door of the hut, leapt to his feet at Adam's words, and ran ahead of them along the path beside the loch. The rain had stopped, and there was a rainbow over the far side of the loch.

'Are we not the lucky ones?' Adam said, pointing to it, 'for I think we have found our own pot of gold, Meg.'

Old Betsy looked as if she thought so as well, her shrewd eyes going from Meg to Adam and then back to Meg again. All she said was that they would both catch their deaths of cold if they didn't get out of those wet clothes right away.

'You were a long time, Meg,' Jeannie said, looking up from her exercise book. 'Could you not find Daddy?'

'It did take me a little while to find him,' Meg said carefully, but she couldn't keep from smiling when she met Adam's eyes.

They decided, that night, that it would be foolish not to tell Jeannie and Betsy right away, although they were both fairly certain that Betsy hardly needed to be told.

'Have you finished your pudding, Jeannie?' Adam said the next night, and Jeannie looked at her father, surprised.

'I've eaten all the custard,' she said quickly. 'It's just one of the prunes I've left.' Reproachfully, she added, 'You know I don't like prunes, Betsy.'

'Aye, I ken that, but they're good for you,' the housekeeper told her, 'but we'll have jelly tomorrow night.'

Adam looked at Meg, and then, reaching across the table, he took her hand in his.

'Meg and I have something to tell you,' he said, and he smiled. 'I think perhaps it will be no surprise to you, Betsy. We're going to be married, Jeannie.'

The housekeeper nodded, clearly satisfied that this was only confirming her own suspicions. Jeannie looked at them, colour slowly flooding her cheeks.

'And then you'll stay here with us for always, Meg?' she asked.

Meg, her throat tight, could only nod and hold out her arms to Jeannie. The little girl's suffocating hug made it all too clear how she felt about the news. A little later Meg, helping Betsy to clear the table, heard Jeannie whisper to Adam, 'Daddy, does this mean that I can give Meg the card I made for Mother's Day?'

'If you want to, lass,' Adam whispered back, and Meg busied herself putting the butter and jam in the cupboard, pretending that she'd heard nothing.

On Sunday morning she had to do more pretending. She lay in bed, listening to mysterious sounds from the stairs and then just outside her door. At last there was a knock.

'Come in,' she called, trying to sound sleepy.

A procession entered. Adam was carrying a tray, Jeannie was helping to balance a small vase with a single rose on it and the two collies brought up the rear.

'It's Mother's Day,' Jeannie said triumphantly, 'and we've brought you breakfast in bed. I did almost all of it myself, didn't I, Daddy?' Then, in case Meg didn't understand, she said, 'I know you're not really my mother until you and Daddy get married, but it's all right, isn't it?'

Meg held out her arms to the little girl.

'It's more than all right,' she said, a little unsteadily. 'It's the nicest thing that's ever happened to me, Jeannie. Oh— and a card for me!'

The large white envelope said MEG in Jeannie's careful printing. Adam held the tray while Meg took the card out. There was a very large heart on the front, and inside the heart were two tall figures and one smaller. And a dog.

'It's us, you see, Meg,' Jeannie pointed out. 'You and Daddy and me and Glen, and you can see he's happy by these marks—that shows his tail wagging. I didn't draw Rex because I didn't have enough time, but I could put him in, if you like.'

Meg assured her that the card was perfect just as it was and, of course, she could see that Glen was wagging his tail.

'You'd better have your breakfast,' Adam said. 'Your muesli is getting soggy!'

He was right, Meg found. Also, the toast was slightly burnt and the tea not very hot. But she meant it with all her heart when she told Jeannie that she didn't think she had ever enjoyed a breakfast more.

She had arranged to have flowers sent to her own mother, and later in the day she phoned her.

'Happy Mother's Day, Mum,' she said. 'I'm sorry I'm not with you, but I'm thinking about you.'

'The flowers are beautiful, Meg,' her mother said. 'Thank you. Now, tell me, how is Jeannie? You said in your last letter she was still in remission.'

'She's doing fine,' Meg replied. From where she was standing in the hall she could see Jeannie in the farmyard, throwing a ball for the two collies.

'I can tell you've become very fond of her, Meg,' her mother said after a moment. 'It must be very hard, not knowing what the future holds for Jeannie.'

Or if there is a future. The words didn't need to be said.

'We do live with that, Mum,' she said slowly, 'but the longer she's in remission the more hope there is.'

There was a silence, and she knew her mother was digesting that 'we'.

'Oh, Mum,' Meg said, unable not to say it, 'Adam and I are going to be married.'

'I'm not surprised,' her mother replied. 'I was beginning to wonder.'

Meg herself was surprised.

'I haven't said much about him,' she said.

'No, dear,' her mother replied serenely. 'It was more what you didn't say. I'm so happy for you, Meg, and so will Dad be. You'll let us know what your plans are, of course.'

That hadn't been a question, Meg knew, and smiled as

she put down the phone. Plans? There hadn't been time, in this wonderful glow of happiness, to think of plans. Just knowing was enough.

That night she and Adam looked in on Jeannie last thing, and Meg tucked the duvet snugly around the sleeping child and retrieved the favourite, somewhat battered teddy from the floor. Outside, on the landing, she looked at Adam.

'My first Mother's Day,' she murmured. 'It's been a wonderful day, Adam.'

She stood on tiptoe and kissed him. It was a kiss that started out to be a light, fleeting touch, gentle and undemanding, but soon Adam's lips were urgent and searching, and his arms held her closer and closer to him. Meg's heart thudded unevenly, and everything in her responded to the demand of his kiss.

It was a long time before they drew apart, unwillingly, but knowing that they had to.

'I think, Meg, we had better be wed as soon as possible,' Adam murmured, his lips against her hair. 'Can I speak to the minister right away?'

As soon as possible seemed a very good idea, Meg, thought, bemused, as she went into her own room.

The next day something happened that added a new dimension to the wonder of their happiness. There was a letter from Dr Robinson in Inverness, telling them of a new drug which had had considerable success with children whose prognoses were much like Jeannie's. He wanted to see Jeannie in a month when he would be able to start her on the drug. There were very few side-effects, he said, and so far the results were very promising.

'He sounds very positive, doesn't he, Adam?' Meg said, rereading the letter.

They decided not to tell Jeannie yet—there would be time enough after the wedding.

'Anyway,' Adam said, 'even the thought of the wedding

is taking second place to the excitement about Glen, working with the sheep again.'

Glen, he said, was as good a working dog as he had ever been. His leg was almost healed, and although he was a little slower than he had once been he had complete command over the sheep. And Rex was learning from him fast.

Somehow everyone in the glen seemed to hear very quickly that Adam and Meg were going to be married, and as Meg went to see her patients or helped in the surgery there were good wishes from everyone.

Betsy began baking the same day Adam went to see the minister.

'It's only going to be a small, quiet wedding, Betsy,' Meg reminded her.

The old housekeeper nodded, and went on mixing another batch of shortbread, watched by Colin and Jeannie.

'Aye, so you say,' she replied, 'but I thought we would just be having a cup of tea and maybe a sandwich or two in the church hall after the ceremony. And my sister is making a wedding cake.'

'I hadn't thought of a wedding cake,' Meg said, a little faintly.

'You canna get married and not have a wedding cake,' Betsy said, in a tone that brooked no argument.

'Auntie Betsy's right, Meg,' Colin confirmed. 'My mum says our Morag has to get a piece of the cake so that she can put it under her pillow, and then she'll dream about the man she's to marry. Our Morag is awful old not to be married, you see.'

Over his red head Meg's eyes met Betsy's, and she realised that Betsy, unlike herself, wasn't struggling to hide a smile.

'Morag is Colin's father's sister, and she's thirty-three,' she told Meg. She looked at Colin. 'And she has to wish, too, when she puts the cake under her pillow.'

Colin and Jeannie moved closer to lick the mixing-bowl.

'The last time Morag had a piece of cake to wish on,' Colin said, carefully licking the spoon Betsy had given him, 'she forgot about it, and the dog found it and ate it so she'll be right pleased to have another chance.'

He looked up as Adam came in the back door.

'Hello, Mr Kerr,' he said sociably. 'Everyone's right pleased that you and Meg are getting married.'

'I'm glad to hear that,' Adam replied, smiling.

'Jeannie and me were just thinking it would be an awful good idea if you could be like Jean Campbell, and have twins. My mum says it's a lot of work, but at least you get it all over at once.'

Meg saw that Adam, like her, was torn between amusement and amazement.

'Well, Colin,' he said, after a moment, 'we haven't got quite as far as thinking about anything like that yet.'

Jeannie put her spoon on the table.

'Well,' she said philosophically, 'you never know, Daddy, you might be lucky.'

'We just might,' Adam agreed gravely. But he had to turn away quickly, Meg saw.

It was a lovely day for a wedding, Meg thought, when she and her father arrived at the small stone church. At last winter seemed to be over and there was a real feeling of spring in the air. As they drove along beside the loch the water lapped against the shore, ruffled by the gentle breeze. There were clouds, but the sky above them was blue—a pale blue, but undoubtedly blue. And there was a gentle warmth in the sun as it kept trying to break through the clouds.

'We do look nice, don't we?' Jeannie said with satisfaction when they got out of the car. She had a new dress, rose-pink velvet with embroidery, which Meg's mother had brought, along with a dress for Meg, which was also rose pink, and silky and swirling.

'Yes,' Meg agreed, and she bent and kissed her almost-daughter. Then, on her father's arm, she entered the church, with Jeannie walking sedately behind her.

The ceremony was short and simple, but Adam's voice was clear and strong as he made his vows and his hand sure and steady when he put the ring on her finger.

It was only when they were outside, and well and truly married, that Meg could look around at the people who had come to wish them well at the start of their marriage.

Her mother and father, Mum happily dabbing her eyes. Betsy, with Colin beside her. Dr Macrae and his wife, and Neil Patterson with them. John Drummond in a wheelchair, with Beth pushing him. Andrew Ritchie, Jean Campbell and so many other patients. Adam's farmer friends—Gavin Ferguson and his wife, Robert Barr and his wife.

People I'm beginning to know well, Meg thought as she and Adam led the way to the church hall. People who would be so much part of her life in the years to come, here in the glen. The glen that already she loved—the loch, the rugged mountains and the gentler foothills, the road that led to the sea. The village itself, and the farmhouse.

But her love for this place was centred and rooted in her love for Adam and for Jeannie. This man and this child. Wherever they are, that is my home, Meg thought with certainty.

There was a piper at the door of the hall, and he began to play as she and Adam reached the door.

'What is it he's playing?' Meg asked.

Adam smiled.

'Well, now, Hector thought that, you being English, it would not be so fitting to play "Marie's Wedding" or one of our Highland tunes. Listen, now, Meg, lass, for I doubt you will ever again hear the wedding march played on the bagpipes!'

The piper smiled and nodded as they passed him, and Meg smiled back.

Arm in arm, she and Adam went in to their wedding reception.

MILLS & BOON®

Makes any time special

Enjoy a romantic novel from
Mills & Boon®

Presents™ Enchanted™ Temptation

Historical Romance™ Medical Romance™

MILLS & BOON®

Next Month's Romance Titles

♡

Each month you can choose from a wide variety of romance novels from Mills & Boon®. Below are the new titles to look out for next month from the Presents™ and Enchanted™ series.

Presents™

THE MISTRESS ASSIGNMENT	Penny Jordan
THE VIRGIN BRIDE	Miranda Lee
THE SEDUCTION GAME	Sara Craven
ONE WEDDING REQUIRED!	Sharon Kendrick
LUC'S REVENGE	Catherine George
THE MARRIAGE TAKEOVER	Lee Wilkinson
THE PLAYBOY'S BABY	Mary Lyons
HIRED WIFE	Karen van der Zee

Enchanted™

BOARDROOM PROPOSAL	Margaret Way
DR. TEXAS	Debbie Macomber
THE NINE-DOLLAR DADDY	Day Leclaire
HER HUSBAND-TO-BE	Leigh Michaels
THE FATHERHOOD SECRET	Grace Green
A WIFE AND CHILD	Rosemary Carter
A REAL ENGAGEMENT	Marjorie Lewty
WIFE WITHOUT A PAST	Elizabeth Harbison

On sale from 2nd April 1999

H1 9903

Available at most branches of WH Smith, Tesco, Asda, Martins, Borders, Easons, Volume One/James Thin and most good paperback bookshops

Spoil yourself next month
with these four novels from

Temptation ®

STRUCK BY SPRING FEVER! by Kate Hoffmann

The Men of Bachelor Creek

Sydney Winthrop wasn't one to back down from a challenge—
even if it meant spending a week in the Alaskan wilderness.
Cold nights, bears, mosquitoes...she thought she was ready for
anything...until she met her guide, Hawk. Hard, lean and
sexy-as-sin, this man was more *dangerous* than everything else
put together!

BLACK VELVET by Carrie Alexander

Blaze

Shy Amalie Dove had caused a sensation writing *very* sexy
stories under the name Madame X. Her true identity, however,
had remained a secret until Thomas Jericho started investigating.
Would he expose her? Maybe...but first he wanted to explore
some of the hidden passions that her writing had revealed...

THE PRINCESS AND THE P.I. by Donna Sterling

Being a billionaire heiress wasn't all it was cracked up to be.
Claire Richmond had had enough of her sheltered life. She
wanted freedom! When Claire did made a break for it, she met
gorgeous, *exciting* Tyce Walker... He seemed to want *her* and
not just her money, but could she trust him?

SINGLE IN THE SADDLE by Vicki Lewis Thompson

Mail Order Men

Daphne Proctor wanted a husband, which was when she saw
Stony Arnett's advert in a magazine. Once they'd met face to
face—and she'd felt the sizzling chemistry between them—
Daphne was sure he was *the one*! But then she discovered that,
though Stony had willingly taken her to his bed, *he* hadn't been
the one advertising for a wife!

FREE
2 BOOKS
AND A SURPRISE GIFT!

We would like to take this opportunity to thank you for reading this Mills & Boon® book by offering you the chance to take TWO more specially selected titles from the Medical Romance™ series absolutely FREE! We're also making this offer to introduce you to the benefits of the Reader Service™—

★ FREE home delivery
★ FREE monthly Newsletter
★ FREE gifts and competitions
★ Exclusive Reader Service discounts
★ Books available before they're in the shops

Accepting these FREE books and gift places you under no obligation to buy; you may cancel at any time, even after receiving your free shipment. Simply complete your details below and return the entire page to the address below. **You don't even need a stamp!**

YES! Please send me 2 free Medical Romance books and a surprise gift. I understand that unless you hear from me, I will receive 4 superb new titles every month for just £2.40 each, postage and packing free. I am under no obligation to purchase any books and may cancel my subscription at any time. The free books and gift will be mine to keep in any case.

M9EC

Ms/Mrs/Miss/Mr ....Initials ....
BLOCK CAPITALS PLEASE

Surname...

Address...

....

....Postcode ....

Send this whole page to:
THE READER SERVICE, FREEPOST CN81, CROYDON, CR9 3WZ
(Eire readers please send coupon to: P.O. BOX 4546, DUBLIN 24.)